ZUMBI,

THE AFRICAN KING OF BRAZIL
A NOVEL

ERICK MAIA

IL
Ivanna Libri
Publisher

Cover design by ebooklaunch.com

Map and Family Tree Illustrations by Andres Aguirre Jurado

ISBN 978-1-7361204-1-5

Before many Black men
Lived and died in America
Here lived and died
Zumbi dos Palmares

CONTENTS

MAP OF PALMARES CIRCA 1655

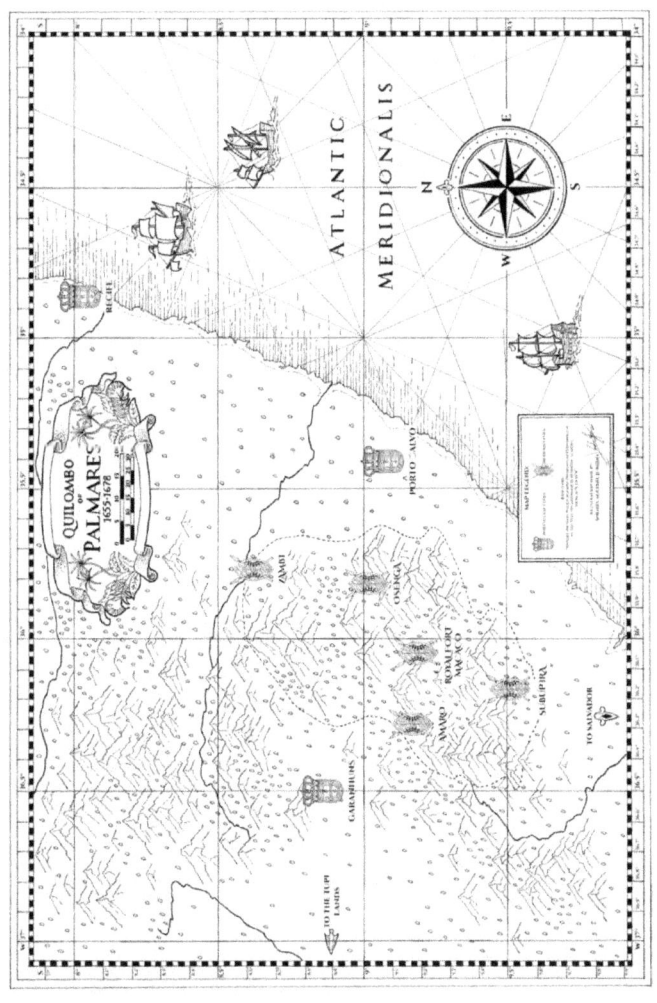

FAMILY TREE

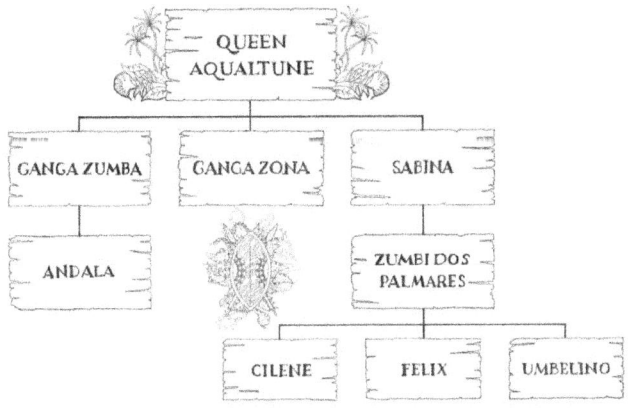

INTRODUCTION

1630
Northeast Coast of Portuguese America, today Brazil

Sugar in the 1600s is like oil will be in the 1900s: a vital, expensive, and rare commodity. Dutch forces invade the provincial capital of Recife, capturing the world center of sugar production from the Portuguese. Enslaved Africans use the ensuing chaos to escape, and the population of runaways living in the hinterland grows.

These communities are called *quilombos*—the African Bantu word for *war camp*.

Palmares is the largest of these quilombos with a population growing to more than 30,000 African men and women living free and independent in the Americas for the first time.

***

1654

After years of skirmishes, battles, and open war, Portuguese forces retake the region and its capital Recife. Now it is time to turn their attention to capturing the Africans back into slavery. After twenty-four years in Palmares, a new generation of Black men and women is being born and raised in freedom.

CHAPTER 1

A NEW HOPE

1655

"Remember that our history starts with freedom in Africa," Queen Aqualtune often said.

Now King Ganga Zumba is repeating it to his council when the scout comes rushing to meet the royal entourage, long fingers of sweat running down his forehead. The royal entourage halts as the lictors—twelve Black men fully armed with swords, bows and arrows, knives, and slings—make space. The king and a few advisors also carry muskets. Prominent among them is Bajes Licutan, royal aide-du-camp, and Palmares's military leader, also known as "The Moor."

The scout kneels down and claps his hands before the king as a sign of submission.

"Our men are all dead, Sire."

Silence falls over the group like a heavy blanket of fog.

King Ganga Zumba looks at the short horizon of the mountain ridge, the tall peaks adorned with the palm trees that gave Palmares its name. He is twenty-five years old and has had twenty-five years of war. Standing at six feet, he is taller than his guards, his lean body marked only by muscles and scars. His skin is the color of a little grape the Native Brazilians bring as offerings and call *jaboticaba*. His long arms are used to fight and his tongue to give command. The voice is deep, with a hint of an accent his mother brought from Africa, where she learned to speak growing up among the Bantu royal family of Angola a generation ago. Ganga Zumba is a handsome African man with a sad gaze toward his enemies' positions amid the tropical trees. He addresses the scout.

"I was hoping you had good news."

"This is the good news, Sire. Not a single one is alive now in the hands of the Portuguese. There is no telling what they would do to make them give away our locations."

"And the bad news?"

"Your brother-in-law was among those killed in battle."

"Sabina's husband? The fool! I told him not to go on this offensive."

"He did anyway, Sir."

Ganga Zumba's gaze floats in the green horizon, his thick lips downshifting, his powerful face heavy with sorrow: a king's sorrow for his subjects fighting for him, for his kingdom surrounded by enemies, for their only chance of freedom. He will carry his pain and the devastating news to his pregnant sister, now a widow and about to give birth to an orphan, like so many. His prominent cheekbones reflect the fading light of the sunset. His pitch-black hair is growing down, weighed by the raindrops that have been sprinkling all afternoon; his hair looks like a lion's mane now. The king looks at The Moor and sighs. His aide remains downcast.

"The women and children?"

"We moved them to the citadel in Subupira. They are now safe."

"As safe as orphans and widows can be in this world," Ganga Zumba says.

"Safe as free people living in your kingdom."

"Our kingdom is now reduced to five citadels spread around this green hell: Amaro, Zambi, Macaco, Subupira, and Osenga. The other settlements are too small to deserve to be called anything else. Five citadels to hold every runaway man and woman in this brutal land where the sun is always setting far from Africa."

His royal guards and entourage, including the twelve lictors who are chosen from among the best African fighters, know better than to push back when the king is brooding on how to continue to resist the Portuguese. His few advisors, including The Moor, also know how to keep their silence. These royal moods always turn around. Eventually. Now, under repeated attacks by the Portuguese forces, these somber moods last longer and longer.

Ganga Zumba turns to the West, his eyes piercing the mountains covered by the green forest that protects them, hiding thousands from European eyes and hands. On the other side, running east toward the coast, are the Portuguese and the Atlantic Ocean blocking the way back, homeward bound to Africa.

"Let us go back to Macaco."

They march back, the sounds of tree frogs and crickets inundating the Atlantic woods in its slopes. They know this is as far as the Portuguese forces will go in offensive movement. These troops will now retreat to Porto Calvo and prepare another attack for the next dry season, their weapons not taking well to the humidity and rainfall of the wet tropical season. These are punishing expeditions, not a conquering operation.

The royal compound of Macaco sits at the center of the main citadel, and this sits at the center of Palmares. The center of the center, his people call it. The palace is a gargantuan wood and clay construction, done in Bantu style, built by master carpenters and masons from Angola, their pride in the craft noticeable in each carved detail. Where the Portuguese only saw brawny arms to harvest sugar, Ganga Zumba saw craftsmen and artisans. These hands built a unique structure with three towers, each supported by Moorish arches as the chief architect was a follower of the Prophet. Each tower is topped by a small religious symbol, as a wooden blessing: one has the Crescent, another the Cross, and the front and central one the Bantu shield—the symbol of African resistance and power.

The large huts around the royal compound are those used by teens since children move out of their parents' house at age ten: one large hut for the boys, another as large for the girls. In front of the compound is the city square, each side occupied by the different temples: one Christian, one Bantu, one Muslim. The outermost ring is composed of single families' houses, each built and occupied by a couple and their children under ten years of age. The only other large buildings are the schools, where the teens spend their days in lessons and training, for life and for war. By the entry gate, the only opening in the tall double palisade is the guardhouse.

This is a community of strong African men, women, and children, as during her reign Queen Aqualtune had little patience for sloth, deception, or weakness. Herself a woman who found her way to freedom while pregnant, she left no latitude toward any form of sloppiness. "Make yourself useful" was her mantra, and that was how she built Palmares, "a paradise out of this green hell." Her attitude shaped their morale, their routine, and organization. It also gave them incredible strength.

She was fond of saying African men are the second strongest people in the world. When asked who was the strongest, she responded with her royal smile, "African women."

As the king's entourage enters the palace, they see courtesans running back and forth, moved by Princess Sabina's labor pains. At the royal kitchen, women, children, and a few men prepare the night's dinner, a banquet to celebrate the dynastic birth. The many scents of food fill the entire village. From one hut, the salty and crisp smell of grilled chicken, corn, and fish, from another the sweet and wet aroma of papayas, bananas, *siriguelas*, pineapples, mangos, guavas, and oranges. This bountiful feast is a welcome departure from the usual fare of "corn, plus one meat and one fruit," and if the baby is a boy, they will even add pork to the grill.

The culinary options of this tropical forest are crafted from traditions and manners dating back to Angola, in Africa, with modifications and adaptations learned from the Tupi customs and the Portuguese cuisine. This African-Tupi-Portuguese encounter in cooking hits the nose with the powerful, delicious, and flavorful smell of palm oil. When the kitchens of Palmares are busy, the smell emanating makes all people wish they could sink their teeth into the world of flavor. When the captured Africans dream on a hungry stomach many a night, their memories take them back to the land of Angola and their African palm oil. That's why when escaping the Portuguese, they can sense direction by the sight and smell of the palm trees surrounding the mountains and Palmares. Those same palm trees provide them with the equivalent oil from the African palm trees. Hence Palmares' power to attract so many: the highest ideals of freedom and the basic need for nutritious food.

Back at the compound, Princess Sabina is serene while others around her appear anxious. The midwives prepare their wares and say their prayers.

"She needs not know right now about her husband's death. I will tell her later," the king whispers to his entourage, then says to himself, "Gods, bring me some good news today."

Kings both want and need good news to share with their people. A prince born into freedom will give the people of the five citadels something to cheer for and, even more importantly for the ruler, something to fight for. Ganga Zumba holds his sister's hand tenderly and speaks to her softly.

"People need something to live up to. Our family crossed the big ocean in chains but we lead these men and women back to freedom in this unknown land." Without a noise he kisses Sabina's forehead. She beams at her older brother.

"Your majesty is our reason for hope," an advisor tries to interject.

"I am. Yet one day when the sun sets, we need to make sure there is a rising sun ready in the horizon."

Sabina's pains and pulse increase. The lead midwife asks the king and his male advisors to leave the room. The king's guards and his captains surround him and they move out. The tall Black men march in lockstep, carrying even taller lances and enormous bows with quivers full of long arrows, their steps resounding on the wooden floor. Their dark skin and massive muscular bodies comprise their only armor.

"In the delivery room, you command the King, madam!" Ganga Zumba says with a smile as they exit and he leaves his sister and hopes behind—both under pain and stress. The midwife is serious as she takes the princess's accelerating pulse and dries the sweat on her forehead.

The king does not go far. With his military advisors, he occupies a nearby room and discusses plans to move a settlement the Portuguese may have spotted.

"Better yet, we set a trap for them there."

A small group leaves with the orders.

Back in the princess's quarter, converted now into her delivery room, the midwives work their art. The prince is born, like all humans, soaked in blood and tears. Unlike others, he is attended by a selected wet nurse and brought directly to the king.

"A healthy baby boy."

A firm Black baby's grip tightens around his uncle's thick finger. To the baby, an uncle; to all others, the king.

Ganga Zumba's laugh seems to occupy his entire face, his pitch-dark eyes shining over his nephew. He takes the baby in his muscular arms and gigantic hands, soothing him with whispering old African words. These are words left in his brain by his mother, the one who had a childhood on African soil, the same one taken in the bowels of a ship to this new land, the one who reminded him he was the son of a queen not of a slave. Like so many moments of peace in this age of war and battle, this one does not last long, just long enough to leave a taste of respite before melting again into reality.

The head midwife comes with clothes and sheet soaked in bright red blood, royal blood.

"My lord, we did all we could. The princess's blood was thin, we could not stop it from flowing out of her body. Our princess is no more. Pardon me."

The head midwife bows down. Her shoulders are heavy with grief. All the other maids bow with her, their faces wet with tears.

Ganga Zumba tightens his arms around the newborn, his muscles creating a barrier to hold reality away from the innocent. He lowers his head, tears and hair falling over the infant. Too much pain for one day, even for a king used to losses and setbacks.

A Royal Proclamation

He approaches the princess's bed and whispers in her ear, "I will take care of your son as my own son." He kisses her forehead gently and touches her hair with his powerful hand. Ganga Zumba then resumes his commanding stance and orders the captain of the guard:

"Call the people. We have a royal proclamation. Tomorrow we have a funeral, but today we have a birth."

The drums sound around the royal compound and a crowd gathers outside, coming to hear their leader and see the princess's offspring. The main drummer, their maestro, is a small Black man by the name of Djavan. He was born blind and to escape the tradition of eliminating disabled Black babies in the sugar plantations, his mother took him in her arms and escaped to Palmares. This little blind child gave her the vision she needed to find freedom.

He grew up in Palmares and since his early days all he wanted was to play with sounds. Deprived of light and images, his powerful mind created castles and kingdoms in the air with music. Although his given name is Djavan, everyone knows him as "Wonder" since only a miracle from the gods would give so much music, rhythm, and lyrical talent to one person. He quickly became their maestro for the nights of Palmares: nights filled with music, songs of freedom, redemption songs.

In front of the royal compound there is a ten-foot-tall stand built with strong *jacaranda* wood for proclamations by the king and his ministers. From their mouths, these words are carried to each village by the quiet whispers of the forest. Now Ganga Zumba takes the steps alone with the baby in his arms, dressed in the royal mantle decorated with green and blue feathers from peacocks and macaws. The sky above is painted red by the sunset unfolding behind the mountains and the dark night advancing from the coast. From the top of the royal stand, the king can see above the green mantle of the forest surrounding them, shades of green floating over the edge of his vision.

"People of Macaco! Men, women, and children of Palmares! Each of you, or your fathers before you, were taken from mother Angola, our land which the pale hands call Africa, and thrown into the deep sea to be taken to this strange land and work until you die. You are orphans of Africa growing up under the whip of these pale hands, full of cruelty and devoid of love.

"We, here and now, have found each other in brotherhood and are no longer enslaved. We are free brothers and sisters in the love we have for one another. We are free by the love we hold for one another. We have found the path to the forest where we are free to toil and prosper. We are no longer orphans because we have one another. We fight and live and work together, protected by the green walls and the towers of mountains.

"I bring you a prince, whose mother died giving him life. Yet he is not an orphan, because of the love we have for one another. As your king I am your father and I present to you our new prince. His name will not be tied to any family or village, for he will be known as Zumbi of Palmares. As your king, I command you to take this baby as your child, a child of the community of free Black hands. A child of Angola born on these shores, free. As your brother, I ask you to take this child and grow him to be a powerful prince. This child will not know what it is like to be a slave in a strange land because for him this land will be his land, your love will be his mother's care, and his duty will be to protect and guide us to remain free and build out of pain, glory; out of defeat, victory; out of exile, a home."

Ganga Zumba looks down and raises the baby toward the sky. His gaze follows, tears and sweat mixing down his stern face. A drop of blood drips down onto his forehead. Blood, sweat, and tears fusing in the Brazilian tropical twilight.

"This prince lost his father in battle today to give us life. This prince lost his mother today to give him life. Yet he is not an orphan. Every man in this kingdom is his father. Every woman in this kingdom is his mother. Every boy is his brother. Every girl is his sister. You too one day were without father and without mother in this godforsaken land. Then one day you ran for freedom and found your brothers and sisters in this jungle. Together we built six citadels surrounded by trees and tucked in these mountains. Five are still standing strong and together we will raise this prince to be king. A king worthy of Africa, of Angola, and of you!"

With each word, his voice gains strength and power. Ganga Zumba, with the little bundle in his arms, concludes with the child's royal welcoming:

With the judgement of the angels and the sentence of the saints, we bless, praise, consecrate, and welcome Prince Zumbi, the whole of the sacred community assenting, in the presence of the sacred books with the 613 precepts written therein, pronouncing for him the benediction wherewith

David blessed Solomon, and all the benedictions written in the Book of Law. Let him be blessed by day and blessed by night; let him be blessed in his lying down and blessed in his rising up; blessed in going out and blessed in coming in. May the Lord forevermore embrace and acknowledge him; may the love and pleasure of the Lord be henceforth placed over this man, load him with all the blessings written in the Book of Law, and write his name across the sky and across the waters of the sea; may the Lord welcome him with love from all the tribes of Angola, weight him with all the benedictions of the firmament contained in the Book of Law; and may all you who are obedient to the Lord your God, to Allah and the Prophet, and to Mpungu and his legions, be saved this day.

The people of Macaco celebrate. Carriers are sent to the other four villages, the forest alive with whispers and hope and the sound of drums and music. Wonder creates a new tune, which he sings with his raspy perfect voice, a song he titles "You are the Sunshine of my Life"

Ganga Zumba's principal advisor is a woman in her forties, about ten years his senior. Probably she is among the oldest people in Palmares, though that exact time accounting is impossible: those enslaved do not have birthdates and calendars are a luxury. They call her Doriana, yet the king playfully calls her Dorine, meaning "gift from God."

"A baby is new hope for our people, Dorine," says Ganga Zumba.

"Yes, it is, my Lord. I know. I remember when you were born."

She looks at Ganga Zumba with tender eyes, beaming quietly while he looks at the baby in his arms with a tearful gaze.

The entire community looks at the three of them by the throne. They are ready to fight, to live another day and many other nights.

Wonder continues to sing and Doriana follows him promising to keep the little prince forever in their hearts.

The past is present in each word, and so is the future.

***

A Mother in Church

Next morning the past resurrects with the sun and the royal family gathers for a private burial ceremony for princess Sabina. Ganga Zumba keeps the baby in his arms all the time, not letting him out of sight unless to be fed by wet nurses. Members of each of the ruling families of the different villages are present: Chiamaka from Zambi, Jaha from Amaro, Lolonyo from Subupira, and Ashon from Osenga. Each offering promises allegiance and support to the baby prince Zumbi. Members of the royal cabinet are also present, including Doriana, The Moor, and Master Yalom—a Jewish Dutch refugee. For a royal family, even these private ceremonies involve a small crowd and multiple interests.

Sabina's diminutive body is taken to the Christian church where it is buried under the first row of seats, where the family prays and kneels together. Her husband, as a warrior killed in battle, will be buried where he fell. It is in this first row that Zumbi will spend all Sundays of his childhood, imagining his mother is there with him, looking at the images of the Virgin and wondering about these white people who killed God only to worship him to the end of times.

The bond between the African son with a dead mother and the Virgin with the dead son is one that will last beyond many battles and the stinginess of the world.

The people of Macaco will make that burial site under the first row in the church a small sanctuary for the young princess Sabina who died widowed and left an orphan to be raised by them as a prince. Out of death, a new life; out of despair, a new hope.

Dutch Interlude: Amsterdam, 1656

As a community twice removed, the newly arrived Portuguese Jewish community cannot afford to harbor heretics. This is an age of intolerance and suspiciousness, and the young scholar has been talking about God having a body and angels being a hallucination. Worse crime, and even worse sin, he proclaims the Bible as metaphorical and allegorical. This is an age of avoiding interpretation and taking all words as literal. To culminate his grave mistakes, he proposes that such literal readings of the Sacred Book lead to errors, contradictions, and impossibilities.

The Jewish elders offer him an annuity in exchange for his external loyalty to their faith and synagogue. He refuses. And so, he's excommunicated in summer.

With the judgement of the angels and the sentence of the saints, we anathematize, execrate, curse, and cast out Baruch de Spinoza, the whole of the sacred community assenting, in presence of the sacred books with the 613 precepts written there in, pronouncing against him the malediction wherewith Elisha cursed the children, and all the maledictions written in the Book of Law. Let him be accursed by day, and accursed by night; let him be accursed in his lying down, and accursed in his rising up; accursed in going out and accursed in coming in. May the Lord never more pardon or acknowledge him; may the wrath and displeasure of the Lord burn henceforth against this man, load him with all the curses written in the Book of Law, and blot out his name from under the sky; may the Lord sever him from evil, from all the tribes of Israel,

weight him with all the maledictions of the firmament con-
tained in the Book of Law; and may all you who are obedient
to the Lord your God be saved this day.

The sentence forbids speaking to him in writing or ver-
bally, forbids doing him any favor or sharing a room with
him. It also forbids reading anything he writes.

He is twenty-four years of age and will live another
twenty-one years. Enough time to complete four books and
change the world. His name is Baruch Spinoza.

Chapter 2

Growing Up in Palmares

1656

At the village of Amaro the Soares family welcomes a hale and hearty baby boy whom they name Antonio. The Soares family escaped the Dutch forces, for they had already been free under the Portuguese government. Among the Africans under Portuguese rule, those able to read and write served as organizers of the trade. With the Dutch occupation the Soares family decided to shelter in Palmares and fell in love with the free republic.

They are now settled at the Amaro village and when King Ganga Zumba sees little Antonio, a boy the same age as Zumbi, he invites him to grow up in the Macaco royal compound. A chance to live in the center of power is welcomed by the Soares family and thus Antonio comes to live with the royal family. That same year Ganga Zumba's wife gets pregnant and delivers another baby boy to Palmares, Andalaquituche, known by all as Prince Andala, born nine months after Zumbi. The three boys discover the world together as friends, like brothers are meant to do.

***

1660

The year has been happy in the village of Zambi. After many years of expectation and false hopes Kande, chief Chiamaka's wife, is to deliver a baby. This time Kande takes all precautions and rests for months. Now with the arrival of the pain, Chief Chiamaka paces back and forth as his midwives attend the delivery. The chief has wanted a boy, an heir to the reins of Zambi. When they bring him the little baby girl all his wishes for a son evaporate and he loves his daughter, planning to make her a suitable ruler.

"Your name will be Dandara, our Black princess, our Black warrior."

Chiamaka's paternal devotion to his daughter remains undiluted as Kande does not conceive again. Dandara's upbringing will combine all the lessons from her mother along with the teachings of her father, including learning capoeira before the regular age of ten. By the time she is a teenager Dandara is a better capoeira fighter than anyone in Zambi, where her father keeps a vigilant eye and where she takes all her education and training. As long as he can he will postpone Dandara's venturing into the world, for he knows what the world does to people. The people of Zambi are fond of saying "Chiamaka rules Zambi but Dandara rules Chiamaka."

***

1663

Eight happy years of innocence follow and childhood passes, and while the adults fight to keep the citadels intact and the Portuguese away, children and nature continue to unfold their hidden potential. What is it like to grow up in Palmares? It is like growing up in any other place, any other time: a miraculous process of playing games and having fun as you are slowly pushed out of paradise. The wet season is followed by the dry season which is followed by the next wet season; the crops grow, are harvested, and are replanted to grow again. By now the Africans know the rhythms of these lands: rain from March through June, the rest of the year dry and hot.

The population of the quilombos increases with new arrivals and even more births, including some Tupi families as well as some Dutch refugees and even a few Portuguese escaping their pale king's justice. King Ganga Zumba organizes and governs Palmares with his advisors, foremost among them Doriana and the Moor. Princes Andala and Zumbi do the work of growing up among courtesans and friends in the royal compound of Macaco. The king's brother Ganga Zona leads the village of Amaro.

In these eight years none of the citadels have fallen and smaller villages are emerging in their shadows, and the population explodes not only in size but also in the belief they can live and prosper as free people on the American continent. Some now call Palmares *Little Angola*—enjoying the sound of their ancestral home one ocean away, feeling the pleasure of saying its name. The king likes to spend time with the three boys and talk about the somber reality surrounding their bright playful days at the palace.

"Even in these sunny green lands there are shadows all around us," Ganga Zumba reminds them, meditating out loud.

***

An Unusual Arrival

Innocent of the shadows, the eight-year-old princes play in the compound when, one sunny day, an unusual man arrives at the gates of Macaco. He is unaccompanied and without the usual marks of pale hands' cruelty that motivated so many to risk limb and life to find freedom in the quilombo. He is already an old man. Such an appearance is bound to elicit suspicion. Is he a spy for the Portuguese? Is he a Trojan Horse prepared to open their gates to the enemy when they are asleep? The suspicions grow wild as he refuses to speak but to the king himself. Because he is an African man, with Bantu accent and Black skin to show for it, they take him to the royal compound.

King Ganga Zumba receives him like he receives any Palmarian citizen, surrounded by his advisors and lictors and, as rulers like to do, goes straight to the point:

"How can I help you?"

"It is me who is here to help you, my Lord."

The advisors have a hard time containing their disdain, all except Doriana who from the moment the strange man entered the room has kept a surprised stare fixed at the new arrival.

"In three months, you will be attacked."

Ganga Zumba always takes a keen interest in any information about potential Portuguese attacks on the villages.

"We are attacked about every other month by small bands of Portuguese farmers looking for their pieces. They call us *pieces*! Every such attack each month has been deflected. Three months will give us time to rest. This is nothing new," says the king.

The advisors laugh to please their king. Doriana and the Moor remain serious. The new arrival continues:

"The attackers will be led by a Black man. This is not going to be an attack by a marauder band, this is an expedition to conquer and destroy."

Now they all get serious and Ganga Zumba stares at him.

"And how do you know that?"

"I was told in a dream."

The smiles come back to the advisors' lips, a result of their fear and relief. All smile except Ganga Zumba, the Moor, and Doriana. There is something about this man's tone that gets Ganga Zumba's attention.

"Thank you, stranger. State your name."

"Hermes Seixas."

"In what direction is this attack coming?"

"In the dream I saw a village whose name starts with a Z or an S?"

"That's Subupira or Zambi. Moor, make inquiries and prepare both villages for a heavy attack."

The Moor leaves the room and dispatches two warning letters with guards, one to Chief Chiamaka and another to Chief Lolonyo in Supubira.

"Hermes, you are welcome to stay in Palmares. You can join the men's hut."

"Sir, I came here to marry and live with my wife."

"You have a wife here?"

"I do." Hermes says without much emotion.

"Do I know this woman?" asks Ganga Zumba.

"Yes, my lord. She is sitting right by your side."

All eyes jump to Doriana, who keeps looking at him with curiosity. Ganga Zumba is the first to break the silence.

"Do you know this man, Doriana?"

She nods slowly, responding with a tentative *yes*.

"How so?"

"He appeared to me in a dream, last night."

Silence went back to the room. Witchcraft is a reality in the Americas as it is in Africa as it is in Europe in these days. Two dreamers can certainly meet in some land where the spirit goes at night when it leaves the body resting. The king turns to Doriana:

"What to do, my trusted advisor?"

After a long silence, which no one in the room challenges, Doriana responds, now with resolution in her voice:

"My king, my lord, would you marry us now?"

A smile emerges in Ganga Zumba's face, turning to laughter:

"Of course."

A quick ceremony follows as the king is used to marrying people as a head priest to the community. The brutal reality in which they live keeps reminding them of the need to make prompt decisions and not spend too much time in ceremonies.

***

Doriana and Hermes left the royal compound that evening and have been together since that day. They start to live quietly together in the hut where school take place, where she teaches her students. She continues to advise the king. Hermes keeps to himself and the books. He is always reading and seldom speaks a word, except to Doriana. Their marriage is a long conversation between the two of them. They seem happy.

While they are setting up their lives together based on their dreams, the Black captain Gonçalo Rebelo, with two hundred soldiers, some Black, some Tupi, under Portuguese orders, prepares his attacks. They seem angry.

In Subupira and Zambi the defenses are reviewed and reinforced. The Moor himself spends time between these villages checking each post, drilling with the troops. The Moor's family is descendent of Berbers and Arabs captured in today's Nigeria—a minority of about fifteen hundred people now. As the main military advisor for Ganga Zumba he is usually at the king's side, and his leadership in military operations goes unquestioned by his lieutenants all the way to each individual soldier. His status as unquestionable commandant is the result of his bravery and his willingness to lead men into battle as the first to go and the last the leave.

The Moor is also a master capoeira fighter and swordsman; he respects archers but his own preference is to engage not from a distance but up close. In his face he carries four deep wounds, parallel lines in his cheeks that mark those that pray to Allah. *Drills tougher than battles make for battles easier than drills* is his motto.

It takes three months for Rebelo's troops to find their way through the woods into the farms and ranches surrounding the village of Subupira.

***

Black Captain Attacking

Even with all the warning and preparation the Subupira defenders and the people of Palmares are confused, disheartened, and demoralized by the sight of Black troops advancing against them. At the farms in the outer ring, they refuse to resist Black attackers until it is too late and the Portuguese troops have entrenched themself on their perimeter.

Dispatches are sent to the Moor and he moves his troops to surround the attackers. Rebelo is a veteran of the war against the Dutch and counters several moves to encircle his troops. The Moor himself leads the attacks to push them back, away from the main villages, away from Subupira. In these open confrontations the Portuguese muskets give a powerful advantage against the Palmares troops using arrows and swords, very few having muskets, and even those with little ammunition.

The Moor works diligently to move the battles to locations where his archers can aim without getting hit by musket fire. It is not easy. Several Palmares defenders are killed by the Portuguese fire, yet after three months of back and forth the attackers start to show battle weariness.

The Moor prepares a final trap for the Portuguese Black troops, one attack so complex in timing and location he has to be in the forefront moving each group at the right time. The arrows and slings soften the Portuguese muskets, and a group of capoeira fighters attack their main formation with swords. The Moor is among them, with his sword at hand and a knife attached to his left arm. He uses his capoeira skills to move and at times he appears to be flying. The Portuguese cannot believe the moves and kicks that hit them hard and fast.

Finally, the Moor is face-to-face with the Black captain himself. They engage each other, the Portuguese troops watching their leader take it to the African military chief. The Palmares troops are also observing and they know the Moor's capoeira skills are second to none; he after all taught most of them how to fight and play capoeira.

At first Rebelo takes out a pistol to shoot but the Moor disarms him with a half moon kick. Rebelo then takes out a knife and prepares to stab when the Moor hits him with a hammer kick to the chin that leaves him on the ground. The fight appears settled for the Moor when the sound of a musket interrupts and the Palmares soldiers see the Moor's face covered with blood. The Moor falls back, his hand holding his head, now dripping blood.

Rebelo stands up and regains his step, the Africans jumping in to rescue the Moor at the same time the Portuguese move in for their leader. In the ensuing melee the Portuguese get their captain back and the Palmares troops remove the Moor from the battlefield. He is taken through the forest, yelling orders and telling his commanders to hold the line. Under loud protest he is taken back to Macaco where he is cared for by Doriana, Master Yalom, and Hermes who use all sorts of arts, sciences, and magic to keep him alive. He survives but his left eye is gone. For the rest of his days his stern face will be defined by that lost eye, reminding all around him there is no limit to the Portuguese cruelty and cowardice.

***

The Moor continues to organize the defensive efforts from his recovery bed. After five months of fights, skirmishes, and open battles the Black captain finally returns to Recife with forty prisoners who are promptly and publicly executed for all to see, especially the enslaved people. Palmares is reminded once again that there is no surrender in the struggle against slavery. If it had not been for the dream warnings of Hermes Seixas, that attack could have spelled the end of Palmares. Since that treacherous attack, there has been only silence.

"And silence from the Portuguese only means they are planning something bigger" says Doriana wearily—and wisely.

Ganga Zumba takes princes Zumbi and Andala to see the sites of the main battles and to visit the village of Subupira.

"Now the Portuguese know the location of this citadel," concludes the king.

"We need to protect it, even more than the others that are hidden," the eight-year-old Zumbi replies.

"You are right, Zumbi. We need to do that."

"How about we surround it with a tall and powerful fence?"

"I like that idea, Prince. I like that very much."

And that is what is done: a stockade is built under the supervision of Bantu engineers and Master Yalom's architecture. Subupira becomes the first official African fort in the Americas. The tall fence with towers and gates in Bantu style is erected, large banty shields decorating the belfry of each tower. African guards and archers are posted in each of these towers, day and night. All over Palmares there is pride about the structure now called Fortress Subupira.

Some in Palmares almost want the Portuguese to try to attack again.

The Occult History of Mountains

As life has since time immemorial, those in Palmares sought refuge in mountains for protection, air to breathe, and sustainable livestock. This goes beyond our story, way back when it all started before the human age.

At the very beginning, the planet is a hot red rock speeding around the Sun trying to cool down. On its surface, all chemicals mix in the mineral kingdom and create the one indispensable life ingredient: water. Life starts simple and in the water. As it grows it is hungry for oxygen and minerals, scant in the aquatic realm. Those early life-forms wait for millions of turns around the sun until the shifting plates collide to form the first mountains.

Mountains take life away from the water and push it toward the sky. As they crumble, their pieces fall back to the primitive ocean. That mix from the heights generates the oxygen and nutrients needed to make life more complex, and thus it grows and keep growing. Mountains give birth to an ever-expanding catalog of animals and peoples.

In the ancestral memory of humanity, we know this. We hold sacred mountains in awe: Mount Athos, Mount Fuji, Mount Sinai, Uluru, and so many others. The Greeks place their gods on Mount Olympus. All over the cool planet, mountains hold life-giving powers and become the dwelling places of human gods and goddesses, a place for heroes and adventurers. We still, to this day, aim to get to that mountaintop.

The life force brewing in mountains continues to swim in fierce competitions. In the tropics, among those heights and forests, also lives the most formidable killer of men and women, then and now: the mosquito. Mosquitoes in the air kill more people than lions on the ground or sharks in the oceans. Inside these deadly squadrons are even smaller killers that can produce all sorts of fevers and maladies. To complete its own life cycle the mosquito will drink human blood and leave in its stream the seeds of death. From these seeds grow the continuous fevers of dengue, the intermittent fevers of malaria, and the remittent fevers of heart infections. For the women the threat is severalfold bigger: their most efficient executioners are the puerperal fevers following childbirth.

In the delirium of a tropical fever one day a man will dream the idea of animal evolution. This is an age in which men and women do not know what causes these illnesses and this sickness, they only see the bodies left in their wake. Nature holds its lethal secrets hidden from human eyes even if in this age the same humans will enhance their eyes with lenses for near and far. It will take generations to unwrap these mysteries. Until then, mosquitoes are to be feared as the harbingers of death in the bad airs of tropical forests, swamps, and marshes.

The Free Republic of Palmares is defended by Muscles, Mountains, and Mosquitoes.

CHAPTER 3

THE EDUCATION OF A PRINCE

1665

Before starting school at the age of ten, the princes Zumbi and Andala learn about Palmares from the king, to them uncle and father. In his time with the boys, Ganga Zumba is fond of talking about the histories and geographies surrounding Palmares. Like every child, they love to have certain conversations again and again.

"There are three people on these lands: the Portuguese, which like crabs stay on the sandy beaches, scratching the coast; the Tupi, who were pushed to the interior by the Portuguese and live in the great plains of the Hinterland; and our people, brought in large ships from Angola by the pale hands to work on their sugarcane plantations."

"So, we live in the center of the world?" Zumbi interrupts as Andala smiles.

"We live in the center of this land."

"Show us where are the lands where these other people live!"

"The coast, crawling with Portuguese, is east of our mountains. East is where the sun rises every morning."

"East! That's where Africa is!"

"Yes, Zumbi. That is correct. Africa is the farthest east, on the other side of the ocean."

"And which direction is the land of the Tupi?"

"The Tupi, who lived all over this land before the Portuguese took it, now settle in the Great Plains, west of our mountains."

"That is where the sun sets into the night." Andala continues before Zumbi can interject.

"That's right, Andala. We live in the mountains in between east and west."

"So, we live in the noontime sun." Zumbi adds and the boys laugh.

"I guess you can say that," answers Ganga Zumba and joins them in laughter.

"How come the Tupi let us have the mountains?"

"It's good for them to have our people between their villages and the Portuguese," says a pensive Ganga Zumba. "We have learned a lot from the Tupi."

"We? Learned from the Tupi? What have we learned from them?"

"To start with, they showed us these mountains. When the first Africans escaped the sugar plantations they did not know where to go, so they just wandered and many were captured back. Until one day some found their way up the mountains, right here where the palm trees are, where Palmares is today. The Tupi were here and allowed us to stay; they saw we were different, not like the Portuguese trying to capture them. They taught us about the fruit and the animals of these lands, they showed us how to use hammocks to sleep above ground. Most importantly, they showed us it is possible to build strong and prosperous communities on this new continent away from the Portuguese farms and cities."

"How did the Portuguese get so strong, uncle? How come they can sail across the ocean, push out the Tupi natives, and enslave and smuggle us from Africa in chains?"

"The Portuguese secret, Zumbi, is education."

"But my friends say education is about memorizing facts and rules that do not make any sense," says Andala.

"That is because your friends are only seeing information. We need to move from information to knowledge and from knowledge to wisdom. Our people will need wisdom to survive with the Portuguese on one side and the Tupi on the other. If we can do that, we will not only survive but thrive," says Ganga Zumba.

"Do the Portuguese have wisdom?"

"They used to. They used to be heroes, crossing the large ocean like no other people had done before. They opened the curtain of the seas and connected the entire world with their caravels. Slavery is corrupting them as much as it is destroying our people. Exploitation of other people's work devours one's soul. What is left is a lifeless carcass."

"And how come they are still so strong?" Zumbi wants to know.

"They may no longer be wise, but they still have tremendous knowledge. This knowledge gives them powerful weapons, smart strategies, and cruel laws."

"So, they use this knowledge to rule over all of us? And over the Tupi too? That is a lot of strength!"

"The pale hands are weak but their weapons make them strong. These weapons were born out of their education so we follow their system to teach our young. That is why we need to make sure you two grow up with information, knowledge, *and* wisdom. That is what you are going to get with the education we will provide you right here. Not only to you two but to all youth in Palmares, boys and girls."

"And how does this system work, uncle?"

"We separate the children according to their aptitudes."

"Aptitude?" asks Andala.

"Aptitude is your natural inclination. Those good with words learn the trivium: grammar, rhetoric, and logic. Those good with numbers follow the quadrivium of arithmetic, geometry, astronomy, and music. And all students learn to fight. Queen Aqualtune decided long ago that we follow the recommendations of a teacher named Plato, whose book required rulers to be philosophers and philosophers to be kings. You will learn to think, to fight, and to lead. You both will become guardians on the path of becoming the philosopher-kings of our people."

"How about those who are not guardians and will not become rulers like you and me, father?" asks Andala.

"They too have their aptitudes. Some are farmers and grow our food; some are ranchers and take care of cows, pigs, and chickens; some are artisans and craftsmen; some are blacksmiths and leatherworkers; some are cooks; some are builders. Each person in Palmares has an occupation. We all have a role to play; remember we are our brother's keeper. And defending our community is key, so all learn to fight, with hands and feet as well as with weapons. For those helping to manage and rule our people the paths to learn are words and numbers, the paths of the trivium and the paths of the quadrivium."

"So, which path am I taking, uncle?" asks Zumbi, with curious eyes and anticipation.

"You are an African prince, and as such, you will take both."

"Me too?" says Andala.

"You too, Andala. You two are the princes of Palmares; you work harder than everybody else. Always. The work of a prince is never completed: there is always something else to do, somebody else to rescue or fight." Ganga Zumba's memory of his mother, Queen Aqualtune, telling him that very message, brings tears to his eyes.

Zumbi's eyes widen and his mouth turns to a smile. Andala frowns for a moment then follows his cousin's enthusiasm.

"Plus, you will have fun learning to ride horses and to fight, both armed as well as in hand-to-hand combat."

"Will we learn capoeira?"

"Yes, Zumbi, you both will learn capoeira too. The days will be very busy with the trivium classes in the morning, the quadrivium in the afternoon, and weapons and fighting in the evening. That is how my mother had me spend my days and that is how you will spend yours. You will live with the other boys, share the life of teenagers in Palmares."

The boys beam with joy at the prospect of learning the African martial arts of capoeira, the series of complex moves, kicks, and punches that confounds the Portuguese and amazes the Tupi.

And so, at the age of ten Zumbi and Andala move out of the royal compound at the center of Macaco to live in the boys' hut for the next five to ten years of training, depending on their test results. Young men live at that boys' hut until their marriage, with a similar hut on the other side of the school square for the young women. Antonio Soares, Zumbi's best friend in the royal compound, moves out with the princes.

***

Pets in Palmares

As they prepare to move out of their parents' hut into the teen hut for school, many children of Palmares find a pet to keep them company. When people do not love other people, they love animals, says Queen Aqualtune with some exasperation. Children who are not yet at the age of love, have pets.

Women and men tame beasts for work while children do it for play. Adults train chickens, horses, cows, and pigs to toil and produce, while children train dogs and cats to love and play. Because dogs and cats are in short supply in Palmares, the children there find pets in the woods, with parrots, budgies, monkeys, macaws, and even snakes making do for their companionship.

The girls are partial to the birds while the boys prefer the monkeys. In this choice Yakini follows her friends and finds a small perroquet covered in blueish-green feathers with a bright red forehead that she calls *Jandaia*. Antonio Soares follows the boys and adopts a small monkey he names *Sagui*. The princes Zumbi and Andala take longer to find the appropriate companion, with Andala finally settling on a green snake that now lives around his neck and arms. One day this snake will be named *Erythrolamprus viridis*, in the Swedish system, but in these lands they are known now as Crown Ground Snakes. Andala feeds his snake frogs he catches around the rivers and streams. At first the other children are scared of it but eventually they get used to its almost noble presence. Andala calls the snake his *Green Shadow*.

Zumbi does not take on pets as he moves out, maybe because he does not have parents to miss or because he wants no distraction from his double share of classes. It will be a few years until he finally does find an animal to share his days and his nights.

***

The Trivium

Royal Advisor Doriana teaches the trivium courses. Her classes start early each morning in a large bantu-style hut that serves as the main library of Macaco, where she lives with Hermes Seixas, her husband, and hundreds of books. On the walls, between the shelves filled with leather-bound volumes copied by hand, there are clay statues of African heroes, their former Queen Aqualtune, and a few Orixás.

"Even our African gods are in exile," she told the artist as he finished her collection.

On the first day of a new class she welcomes her students with a stern look which makes the class sit in respectful silence and expectation.

"Welcome to the power of words. You are here because of your aptitude in reading and writing. But to date you have been only dating words and sentences, just holding hands. Here you are going to learn to love them properly, make love to them"—the students giggle—"and procreate ideas so beautiful and so powerful that other men and women will follow you. Words are the tools of leaders."

The room's eyes are now glued to her movements, the ears fixated on her voice, hanging on each word, carried by her careful inflection. They see and hear and feel the power of words in action.

"I have here five books we will study in this season, and you will copy each word, in each line, each page of them. The copies you have were made by the students from previous classes. The copies you make will be used by future students. Each year we even create extra copies and spread them across each village."

"Which books are these, Lady Doriana?" asks one of the girls sitting attentively in the first row.

"Good question, young lady. That shows curiosity. And curiosity is the best advice to the young. What is your name?"

"I am Yakini, from Amaro."

"Yakini, that is a powerful name. Tell the class its meaning."

"It means 'truth' in Swahili."

Doriana breaks her stern look in a broad smile. Zumbi looks at the inquisitive student along with the other boys. Young Yakini is short, with thick legs and large hips. She has deep green eyes and the boys have been dividing their short attention between the teacher's words and Yakini's looks since they came into class and saw her sitting in the first row.

"For Latin grammar we read Cicero and Seneca. For rhetoric we read Plutarch and Aristotle's treaties on rhetoric and poetics. For logic, Aristotle's *Organon*, of course."

The students look at the five books and their thick note-books, marked *Grammar*, *Rhetoric*, and *Logic*.

"Go read, copy, and discuss the first chapter of each book. We do not have a printing press yet, so you are it! And remember to write neatly; your scribbles will be the books of the next cohort of students."

The students pick up their piles of books and go out to copy and discuss them in small groups.

"We shall discuss them as a whole class tomorrow. As Aristotle reminds us: *I say that habit's but a long practice, friend. And this becomes men's nature in the end.* I will see that careful use of words and impeccable logical thinking will be your nature in the end."

Sitting next to Zumbi, Antonio Soares whispers to his ear:

"Let us hope these chapters are short."

Zumbi looks instead at Yakini and smiles. She walks past the boys on her way to the girls' quarters. Antonio Soares continues, not paying attention to her as she walks by.

"Come on, princes. We can go play after we finish copying these!" says Antonio.

"Andala and I will sit in on the quadrivium classes as well," says Zumbi.

"Oh boy!"

Hearing that, Yakini stops cold.

"You two are going to sit in on both courses? Learning the trivium *and* the quadrivium at the same time?"

"My uncle—" Zumbi starts.

"That's so smart" she says, only needing these two words to understand.

Her two words echo In Zumbi's mind and make him smile as he and Andala walk to the quadrivium hut.

***

The Quadrivium

The quadrivium courses are taught by a Jewish scholar whose name is Baruch Yalom; we have already met him as Master Yalom, as he is known around Palmares. Master Yalom escaped from Recife where he had been part of that city's first synagogue faculty. As the Portuguese troops advanced over Recife, this community faced a difficult decision: return to Europe and the festering religious wars or sail North, which some Jewish families did, to create a New Amsterdam in the new world on an island they would buy from the natives. The rumors were wild all over Recife, most talking about the natives selling an "island of many hills" and how it was a bargain. In the natives' language they called it *Manhattan*.

Baruch Yalom was tired of fleeing one place for another, so he chose neither, instead moving inland to live among the Africans in the free republic of Palmares. During his work in the synagogue he had lost his faith and realized that without faith, crossing the oceans is much harder. He would not regret his decision. In Palmares, his knowledge of mathematics and astronomy now makes him the natural teacher for the quadrivium, a position he cherishes that makes him known to all as "the Master of Numbers." The precision of his calculations about days and months as well as fences and buildings impressed Ganga Zumbi and his court very much and very early.

At the quadrivium class Zumbi sits in the front row with Andala. He is looking for books and with some relief only sees two volumes on the teacher's desk.

"In these courses on the quadrivium you will have only two books for all four subjects. The first is Euclid's *Elements*."

"Are we copying them too?"

Master Yalom looked at him with a whimsical smile.

"Different from the arts of words in the trivium, here you will not copy anything. You will understand nature, the precise quality of numbers and the universe. As Euclid said: *The laws of nature are but the mathematical thoughts of God*. Here, I will show you how truth lies in that saying. And after seeing that truth, your eyes will be open to the universe."

Next to the books on the desk sits a pile of wooden squares.

"Come look."

The students gather around and Master Yalom lines up four squares on one side and three squares on the other. He then connects them in a ninety-degree angle. He marks the lines and asks the class, "Look here, we have two sides of a triangle, one measuring four and the other three. Question: how long is the third side?"

The students stare at him, mouths shut. Even Zumbi and Andala are quiet.

Master Yalom proceeds to place more wooden squares on the table. The side with four squares now has four lines, each with four squares, for a total of 16 squares. The side with three squares now has, after adding three lines with three squares each, a total of nine squares.

"You now went from seven squares forming the sides of the triangle to twenty-five," says Zumbi, alone among the students.

"That's correct, Prince. I've squared those sides: four squared is sixteen, and three squared is nine."

"But the third side cannot be twenty-five; that is too big."

"That is true, so what is the opposite of squaring a number?"

"You take the square root!" one of the students yells from behind.

"The square root of twenty-five is—"

"Five!" the same student responds.

"And that is the answer. The big side of this triangle is five. It is five here, in Angola, in Portugal, in Holland; it will always be five. Today, yesterday, and tomorrow, it will remain five. These are universal laws; these are the thoughts of God."

The class seems mesmerized and remains quiet.

"You will learn how this calculation is made at the end of the first book of Euclid's *Elements*. And there are thirteen such books!"

Master Yalom, not without some effort, controls his enthusiasm and shows them the second book.

"The second text is Aristotle's *On the Heavens*."

"Aristotle, again?" reacted Zumbi to his classmates' surprise, he and Andala the only ones who had been at the trivium class.

"Aristotle is the base of all thinking in human history," replies master Yalom, unfazed.

"But why? Why are all these authors white men? Who is the Aristotle of our people? Who is the Aristotle of Africa?"

"Aristotle is. Aristotle is the Aristotle of our people. His work is so wondrous it does not belong to the Greeks alone, or to the white people alone. Such a complete work of understanding belongs to all humanity. That is why I am here today, a Jewish Dutch scholar teaching you, an African Prince, about Aristotle. The great Italian poet Dante called him the master of those who know."

***

That night Zumbi has a sleep full of dreams in which books, Yakini, Master Yalom, and Doriana tumble into each other in the dark corridors of his mind. Over them all is written the name of Aristotle, then numbers float in the air. The dream continues with sounds of Portuguese guns upon them all. Zumbi jumps out of his hammock covered in sweat, wanting to command those words and lead his people, to take the initiative, and to beat the Portuguese at their own game of war.

***

Doriana's Library

The next morning in Doriana's classroom Zumbi stays behind until all the other students leave and they are alone.

"I noticed there are more books at your library than those we will read and copy."

"The word is out to the plantations that we welcome books in our quilombo. So now our men, our brothers, which the Portuguese held enslaved, are escaping and bringing with them books. Each book is brought to me and filed, and I organize this library as a central collection right here at Macaco and distribute the extra copies across the other villages."

Zumbi smiles, his eyes running through the titles in the spines, his hand touching the leather.

"Are they all in Latin?"

"Most of them are. The Dutch farmers had some in Greek and Hebrew. There are very few in Portuguese or even a couple in Dutch."

"Can you read in all these languages?"

"Greek and Latin I can. Master Yalom is teaching us, me and Hermes, Hebrew now."

"May I see them?"

"Of course! I am so happy when one of my students takes an interest in our little library."

Homer, Aeschylus, Sophocles, Euripides, Aristophanes, Herodotus, Plato, and Aristotle comprise the top shelf. Zumbi's fingers caress each volume.

"These are our Greeks." Doriana whispers.

The next shelf reads: Julius Caesar, Lucretius, Epictetus, Marcus Aurelius, Plotinus, Virgil, Plutarch, and Tacitus.

"These are our Romans." Doriana continues.

"You say they are ours? These are all white men in robes and many of them enslaved others."

"Yes, they did. And one of them, Epictetus, was actually a slave himself. But slavery in the ancient world was not based on the color of one's skin. That is a modern creation. And it is to justify this abomination that they created the idea of different races and racism. We are different tribes, but as one race we all share more than we differ. By reading these great authors you will learn and be better, and our people and our tribe— which now has an African king and subjects that are not only African but also Tupi, Dutch, and even Portuguese—may prosper."

"Why do we have to be open and welcoming to everyone if they enslave us in return?"

"So that somewhere there exists a tribe based in love and care instead of prejudice and hate. Some societies and ages have a veneer of love and hope covering an underbelly of hate and despair. Some, like Palmares, offer the opposite. Queen Aqualtune gave us the command: *do good to as many people as you can for as long as you can.* That is how we organize Palmares. My husband tells me that is the only reason God does not destroy this wicked damned world."

Starting that night, Zumbi comes from his quadrivium classes back to Doriana's library and takes books to read. He reads for pleasure as he feels more at ease among the words than among the other boys. Even after the strenuous fighting and weapons classes, he swims in the river for a while but returns to spend time in the library with the books, as long as the sunlight allows and night has not closed the eyes of the day. Sometimes, he ends up using a small candle to finish a chapter. Or two.

At the end of his education he will have read all the books in Latin, his first language, and started learning Greek. His favorite book is Julius Caesar's *Commentaries on the Gallic Wars* where he encounters the first emperor's martial style of writing. For the rest of his life he remembers its opening line:

All Gaul is divided into three parts, one of which the Belgae inhabit, the Aquitani another, those who in their own language are called Celts, in our Gauls, the third. All these differ from each other in language, customs and laws.

And he daydreams of one day, when he as an old man will write his own memoirs he will call *Commentary on the Brazilian Wars*. It will start: *All Brazil is divided into three parts, one of which the Portuguese inhabit, the Tupi another, those who in their own language are called Angolans, in Portuguese Africans, the third. All these differ from each other in language, customs and laws.*

During these days Doriana is working on her own book she will title *Wit and Wisdom from West Africa*.

***

The First Trivium Test

To demonstrate how much they have learned, to each other and to themselves, Doriana makes each student go in front of the class and present a topic, any topic, as long as it uses flawless logic, rousing and contagious rhetoric, and correct grammar. Zumbi is the first to volunteer; he steps to the front, faces his classmates, and starts:

"They say my mother is Princess Sabina and before her, her own mother Queen Aqualtune. They say my uncle is King Ganga Zumba. I say no! My mothers are these women

43

who raised me, my father and my uncle the men of Palmares who protect me.

"They say you are escaped slaves shivering and trembling in fear in the green forest. They say your arms are made to grow sugarcane. They say your hands and feet are made for bondage. I say no! You are princes and princesses, you are kings and queens, robbed of your land by evil pale hands. You are Black skin and red royal blood of Africa chosen by destiny and by providence to people this new world.

"They say you must submit and bow. They say you are weak and stupid. I say no! You are artists and artisans, you are engineers and doctors, you are soldiers of the free kingdom of Palmares. You are here to show that the African seed can and will add to this soil, these waters, and this air.

"They say you are poor; I say no! If I am a prince you are my brothers and sisters and you have royal blood running in your veins. They say you are afraid; I say no! You are brave and ready to fight. You have been brought here by an evil hand and here you are born again, in fire and blood, the new sons and daughters, the new queens and kings of a new continent. Thus, laying the foundations of a new world."

The class listens to each word, mesmerized by the gripping rhetoric. This speech will be known and repeated throughout the villages and through the years. It will become legend and be remembered by some as the "I say no!" speech and by others as the "Princes and Kings" speech. The speech is repeated by the parents to their children and taught to the new arrivals as a welcome message about Palmares.

Doriana finds nothing to correct: the logic is clear, the grammar is flawless, the delivery authoritative and caring; it is only the world, the obstinate and stubborn world, that remains to be corrected.

***

Applying the Quadrivium

One rainy afternoon, when the weapons and combat classes get delayed because they are held in an open field, Zumbi lets the other boys go play and stays behind with Master Yalom.

"I have a question," says Zumbi with his traditional princely assertiveness.

Master Yalom is rearranging the rules and spheres used in the day's lecture.

"Of course."

"I understand the uses of the trivium subjects in helping our leadership with words that get others to follow us. How about these numbers and geometries? How are they going to help me do my job of leading?"

The aging Jewish man remains quiet for a bit.

"In leading squads through the forests and fields, is it helpful to know where the directions are?"

"Yes"

"My prince, how do you know where the North and South directions are located?"

"That's easy: the sun goes up in the east and goes down in the west, so if you have your right hand where the morning sun is, or in the afternoon if you have your left hand where the sun sets, you are facing North and your back is to the South."

"Very well. And how do you do that at night?"

Zumbi was taken aback by that very simple question and he could not find an answer. Any answer.

"Look here," says Master Yalom, "you see this big constellation right here?"

"The one the Portuguese call the Southern Cross?"

"That one. Now imagine a line joining the two stars at the head and the bottom of this gigantic cross. Extend the line out another four lengths from the foot of the cross to the south celestial pole. Then look straight down from the south celestial pole to the horizon. There you will find south. Now put your back to it and you are back in control of the four directions."

Zumbi looks at the sky with wide eyes. One can see the wheels turning and that piece of knowledge storing itself for future use.

"I can find my way day and night," he says.

"Yes, you can. That's how our studies of astronomy can create a map in the sky that will serve as a map to guide you on land or sea."

"How about all those operations with numbers?"

"Numbers will be your tool in managing your forces, calculating how many arrows you will need for the number of archers you have, calculating how many rations you need for your troops, even calculating the reach of your slings and the angles for your bows. Operating with numbers, one can get close to predicting the future, and predicting the future is the first step in creating it."

"Thank you. That helps a lot. Next year tell this to the students in the first class. One final question: I see you working with our smiths a lot? What are you doing with these artisans?"

Master Yalom smiles and nods.

"You pay attention to those around you. I am glad you do. I do work with the blacksmiths quite a bit. They are working with the iron ore we trade with the Tupi. They are bringing more and more. Our blacksmiths can forge cast iron and some can forge wrought iron. Cast iron is very, very strong but it is brittle: it breaks. Wrought iron can be bent but it is soft. We are working to get the iron to the middle point. If only we can find the way to stop cast from going all the way to wrought."

"Like Aristotle's doctrine of the mean?"

"Yes, Zumbi. I am glad the trivium classes are teaching you that. You see how our knowledge comes together? This middle point is what we need. Something right between cast and wrought iron. Something that is hard but bendable, something that can be sharpened."

Zumbi is following each word, his mind making the connections. He can almost see that middle point and how useful it would be.

"This forged metal in the middle point would be great for knives and swords. We could get them thick and sharp at the same time."

"Yes, prince. We need it. With weapons made with that perfectly created metal we will have weapons to counter the Portuguese muskets."

"How do you call that middle point between cast and wrought iron?"

"That, prince, is steel."

And that's how Zumbi's curiosity helps him learn about Master Yalom's special project with the smiths and their forges. Now the classes do not sound so abstract and at times pointless. Now Zumbi understands why as a prince he needs to make all these connections. He tries to convince his friends of the importance of learning but by now the boys have eyes and minds devoted to the young women around them.

Next day Zumbi goes on and on about types of iron with Acirema who listens to him, enchanted. At the end Zumbi jumps from the need for finding that middle level between cast and wrought iron to conclude for her, and for himself:

"That is the type of leader Palmares needs, and I should be. A leader made of steel, who can bend but not too much like wrought iron, and be hard but not brittle like cast iron. We need a leader made like steel. That is it."

French Interlude: Castres, France, 1665

January 11—He is feeling ill and tomorrow he will die, leaving behind a riddle that will haunt mathematicians for decades, then centuries.

His fame was acquired, at the age thirty-five, by the discovery of a friendship nobody had noticed before. The friendship between 17,296 and 18,416. Wise men for centuries had known of the love between 220 and 284, and nobody suspected another pair of amicable numbers would be waiting to be found somewhere in the infinite tapestry of numbers.

The love is demonstrated by the divisors of 220—1, 2, 4, 5, 10, 11, 20, 22, 44, 55, and 110—summing up to 284, while the divisors of 284—1, 2, 4, 71, and 142—sum up to 220. This pair of enamored numbers were so symbolic of friendship that talismans with them were sold in the Middle Ages to promote love. An Arab numerologist went further and suggested carving 220 on one fruit and 284 on another, then eating the first one and offering the second as a love-philter. The pair 220 and 284 was held as unique until he brought forth the lovebirds 17,296 and 18,416.

He then proceeded to tease mathematicians by arguing he had proof that 26 was very special indeed as the only number to live between a perfect square, 25 (5 x 5), and a perfect cube, 27 (3 x 3 x 3).

His last mischievous riddle was scribbled in the margin of a book and starts with Pythagoras's theorem, in which:

$$x^2 + y^2 = z^2$$

He took one step further and considered $x^3 + y^3 = z^3$ and realized it had no solution. He moved to 4 then to 5 and kept getting no solutions. Only squares summed to squares. He then scribbled as a side note in his copy of *Arithmetica*:

> *It is impossible for a cube to be written as a sum of two cubes or a fourth power to be written as the sum of two fourth powers or in general for any number which is a power greater than the second to be written as a sum of two like powers.*

To make the puzzle even more tempting and maddeningly irritating to mathematicians, he added the following:

I have a truly marvelous demonstration of this proposition which this margin is too narrow to contain.

He is sixty-three years of age and his name is Pierre de Fermat.

CHAPTER 4

CAPOEIRA:
LEARNING TO DANCE AND FIGHT

"It is a dance!"

"No, it is a fight!"

Zumbi and Antonio Soares enjoy sparring about everything like two children who are also best friends growing up together, discovering the world, one dispute at a time. Prince Andala, a few months younger than both, and always the junior partner, keeps on watching them.

"If it is done with music, and follows a rhythm, it is a dance!"

"I have seen how they can dismount an opponent with a half moon kick! So, it is a fight."

"It is a dance, you just do not have ginga! If you had ginga, you would know it is a dance!"

They are finally now ready to attend the first class of weapons training and hand-to-hand combat. The Moor himself is coming to give them an important introduction on the importance of mastering the martial art of capoeira.

"He always does the first opening class," says Yakini, who seems to know everything.

The children sit in a large semicircle, all ready to start jumping and kicking and throwing arrows and spears. The Moor comes in, his slim muscular body showing multiple scars as he removes his shirt.

His opening line is: "Capoeira will prepare you for the greatest fights you will ever have to face: us against the Portuguese and boys against girls!"

They laugh, as they have never seen their military leader crack his stern commanding look.

"In the Palmarian army, our African army in the jungle, we are all one. We all fight for you and you will fight for us all. We need to leave all pretense at the door. In battle I do not care about your rank or age; I care that you do what you can to win, and I will do the same for you.

"When our ancestors were enslaved by the Portuguese, they needed to practice their fighting techniques. But the Portuguese would not allow for any such practice in the slave quarters. So we invented capoeira. We told them it was a dance and they believed it. They allowed us to practice because they could hear the music and it was pleasurable to their ears. Their eyes became blind to the strength and the speed those enslaved were developing. Until it was too late!"

The Moor signals one of the soldiers to start marking the rhythm using the berimbau. The tempo is catchy and the children become enrapt in the music, repeating itself after so many short phrases.

Bing … Bing … Bing … Bing, Bing, Bing, Bing.

The sound seems to repeat the name of the instrument: berimbau, berimbau …

Then the Moor starts to move, back and forth, back and forth, forming a large X on the ground with his steps. Back and forth he goes. Then suddenly he jumps in the air, his whole body moving as if pulled by invisible strings in the open air: he is airborne. He lands behind the children then moves again, back and forth, back and forth, and jumps again to the front, again becoming airborne in front of their enchanted eyes. At one point he lands on one hand and keeps his feet in the air, defying gravity, then pushes himself backward with that one arm and lands back on his feet, staring at them.

"You may run out of ammunition for your musket, you may run out of arrows in your quiver, but your arms and legs are with you always.

"Remember to do something! Anything! Just do not freeze in combat. That's the worst that can happen. We need to give you ways to react so that you will never freeze. "Sometimes people talk about the choice between fight or flight. These are not the only options. These are not even the most common options. Most people freeze! And that is when the Portuguese will get you. Do not freeze. Do not freeze, I repeat. We will give you ten techniques you can apply, one hundred ways you can run, so that you never, never ever, freeze!"

They have to spar with each other, girls and boys mixed in each group. Princes Zumbi and Andala, along with Antonio Soares and Yakini, remain inseparable. They sit together in the circle, practice together, and thus spar together.

Sparring then becomes their one venue for open disagreement and a place where they can attack each other. In friendship and in the trivium classes, and for the princes the quadrivium classes as well, they share the magic of learning and discovery. Here in these martial arts classes they learn the limits of the human body, the natural skills of some, the natural clumsiness of others. Antonio Soares and Andala are clumsy and compensate by training extra hours and pushing their muscles to become stronger. They have strength with little speed. Zumbi and Yakini have speed and are natural fighters. They are light and elegant, looking more like dancers.

Still they spar and the results of these encounters are never predictable. There are times when strength beats speed as much as there are times when speed beats strength. They debate which is better endlessly. What they eventually discover is that it does not matter. If one can control the fight, one will win. If one loses control, one loses. Control is key and controlling oneself is the most important—and hardest to manage—skill. Then one can start controlling the fight itself. If one can make a skilled fighter resort to strength, that fighter will lose. If one can make a strong champion try a skillful technique, a mistake is likely to ensue and so is an opening. It is all about control. And the paradox of control is that one only has it when they give it up.

They persist. They practice six days each week as a group. Even on Sundays, the one day reserved for resting, sometimes they go into the forest and look for a clearing in which to spar. By year's end, the four of them are the best capoeira fighters in their group. What they cannot decide is which one is the best among themselves. Their friendship in the end is the best. They remain friends. Winning and losing.

There are many stories about the adventures of Yakini, Andala, Antonio Soares, and Zumbi that will be whispered as legends through African tongues in America for years to come. These adventures include challenges and trials they had to overcome with the power of their capoeira skills and their weapons. In the end it was clear to all: their friendship was the one power they needed to overcome each obstacle.

***

Weapons Training

Despite the arms and legs powered by capoeira, weapons skills are still much needed. And those who wield the weapons of Palmares are divided into three teams: those of close contact, using swords and knives; those of distance aim, armed with slings and arrows; and the very special muskets team. Here again all students learn the basic skills and depending on their inclinations they end up in teams of fighters training with close and distant weapons. The boys tend to prefer the swords and knives teams, the girls the slings and arrows. Muskets are reserved for those with good aim. Due to their royal roles Zumbi and Andala are issued muskets. Ganga Zumba has had them training on muskets from a young age, so they both learned to shoot well.

Here Zumbi and Yakini break the mold as he excels in the slings and arrows while she has the natural moves for fencing. So when it comes time to divide the team, Zumbi falls onto the "girl team," for which he is teased by his friends in the boys' hut, while Yakini joins the "boy team" of swordfighters. They do not care, for he loves his bow and sling and she adores her knives and swords.

After the general training in capoeira they go to their team arenas and practice. Quickly Zumbi masters the arrows and soon they are moving targets and elaborating complex shooting challenges. The slings are harder to aim and prove the harder weapon to use. There are rumors Master Yalom is working on a special sling bullet but those for now are only rumors. For their practice they pick up bags of river stones from nearby streams and creeks.

CHAPTER 5

A PRINCE'S FIRST LOVE

How does a prince fall in love? Is it through the eyes, by seeing the beautiful girl on the way to the school hut? Is it through the smell of this girl as she works washing the sheets and clothes of the women's hut? Is it through the ears, by the sound of her innocent laughter, so free of care and worries that it sounds like the first cry of a child seeing their mother? Is it by noticing how different she is from the courtesans inhabiting the royal house? And why is it that despite all those beautiful courtesans and cousins, he falls for another girl, one who lives far from the palace corridors and the court mores and traditions?

Each day as Zumbi passes from the boys' hut to his classes he tries to catch a glimpse of this girl. When their eyes meet something shakes in his chest, something new, something good. Every day that this happens, the same emotion makes him smile to himself. Every day when he fails to see her, the same disappointment bleeds into his day, making it a little less interesting. By careful asking, he learns her name is Acirema and she is the daughter of Tuibae, a Tupi blind man who one day sought and found refuge in the quilombo.

And every night as Zumbi lies in his hammock, the same question haunts his mind to sleep: Does she feel the same about me?

Were he better acquainted with the arts of love, he would recognize the same spark in Acirema's eyes.

Antonio Soares, who has had encounters with love, recognizes Zumbi's interest in the girl and asks:

"What do you want to know?"

"I wonder how come her father needed refuge in our quilombo?"

"Because we needed a translator. He is our walking Tupi dictionary."

"That is why we needed him. Why does he need us?"

"I do not really know. You ask too many questions." Antonio Soares knows Zumbi never gives up on getting answers to his many questions. It is one of his many princely traits: he always wants to know and he does not let go of questions.

"I just want to know."

"You can go ask him."

Like the other times when he has had a question, Zumbi will not rest until he finds an answer. A few days later, he works quickly on his school tasks to find time to speak with Tuibae. They are alone by the small hut the old man shares with Zuleika, his African wife, and Acirema, their daughter. The women are out gathering food then will be preparing the night's meal. Zumbi finds Tuibae sitting outside holding a long cane. They have plenty of time to talk undisturbed.

"Greetings Tuibae."

"My prince!" Tuibae salutes Zumbi yet keeps looking straight ahead.

They sit next to each other on the bench by the door of Tuibae's hut.

"I want to ask you a few questions."

Tuibae nods, looking pensive, still straight ahead.

"Why do you live among us, not among your people?"

A hint of sorrow covers the old man face, which grows sadder.

"People move from their land when their land no longer wants them. People are then pushed out and they become wanderers. I am like a tree without roots. The rain washes me away through this world's streams without end."

"But why?"

"Do you have time to hear my story?"

"I want to know."

***

Tuibae's Story

"I trust you can see that I cannot see with my own eyes. But I hear well and suffer like any other man. When I became blind many years ago my guide was my only son. He became my eyes when my eyes could no longer digest the light. He would hold my hand and carry me here and there. He would go out and find us food. He took care of me. Our Tupi tribe helped us too and we lived with the people. But he was my guide. My son."

Zumbi looks at Tuibae now with a new understanding of his strange gaze lost in the distance. Now he knows that gaze is lost into another kind of darkness, the darkness of longing for a place and a time that no longer exists. Tuibae is only the second blind person in Palmares, after Wonder the maestro. Tuibae clears his throat and continues his story.

"One day war came to us. The fearsome Timbiras attacked our tribe. We lived in dread and as a blind man I stayed with the women while my son went to battle with the other Tupi warriors. The Timbiras are savages, barbarians, but they too have honor and courage. The battles were to the death—on both sides. Anyone captured by them alive was taken to Timbira village, fattened for a moon, then taken to the center of their encampment … to be eaten."

Tales of cannibalism among the natives had been heard around the quilombo, but Zumbi had always thought these were stories to scare children and prevent them from getting lost in the woods.

"The captured warrior has to right then demonstrate his bravery and courage in the face of death. It helps, in this moment, that we believe being eaten by other warriors is much superior to be eaten by worms under the earth. The honorable place to lie dead is in the belly of your enemy, we say."

Tuibae gets excited with his own story, his words falling on each other, while Zumbi, disturbed by this tale, considers the wisdom of getting into Acirema's past.

"The prisoner is taken to their encampment all tied up and has to come in screaming 'here is your food … jumping!' The children and women welcome him by pelting him with fruit and pebbles and saying "We are going to eat you!" to which he responds "I have eaten your cousins and uncles!" The captive is then set free to await his fate. Because escaping is inconceivable, nobody runs away and nobody has to watch over captives.

On the day of the banquet, the whole tribe gets drunk with cauã—their most powerful and inebriating drink—and the prisoner is shaved then painted with herbs and spices. He is then taken to the center of the tribe where the person who captured him will ask, for the whole tribe to hear, "Are you our enemy?" to which the prisoner responds "Yes! I am!" This is answered by "So, we will eat you!" and the prisoner responds "You may eat me but my tribe will come here and eat you too!" All this to demonstrate our courage and bravery. The executioner then comes from behind, with the heaviest of clubs, and with one hit to the back of the head takes the prisoner down. Give me your hand."

Tuibae takes Zumbi's hand and places it on the back of his own neck. "Here, one hard hit right here and the captured man is done." Zumbi withdraws his hand in haste.

"The old women then come by and get all the blood to be drunk while still warm. Then the body is boiled and roasted to be shared by all. Tongue for young men, head for the fiercest warriors, other parts for the women and children."

With wide eyes, Zumbi asks, "Is this how your son died?"

"No. My son had an even worse fate."

"What can be worse than this?"

"Shame. My son ran away. He was afraid. He was worried about my fate as a blind old man without a living child. My son came back to me and when I touched his skin I felt the paint and the spices. I felt his shaved body. He had been ready to be eaten and he had escaped. He ran! My shame was all-consuming. I shed tears for my son's cowardice. He said he had escaped to take care of me! I would much rather starve to death as an old blind man than to have a son run from his warrior fate! I told him this and I cried with humiliation."

"What did you two do then?"

"We both returned to the Timbiras who called my son I-Juca-Pirama meaning 'who must be killed,' but now they did not want to kill or eat him anymore. The chief of the

Timbiras said that if they did, his warriors would become cowards like my son!"

Silence lingers between the two. Tuibae's blind eyes are now marred by tears.

"He then fought the whole tribe. Alone. To show his courage and bravery. He fought so fiercely the Timbira's chief agreed to sacrifice him. I cried again, this time with pride. And I left them with my son, now a dead man despite still being alive. It was then, at that moment, that I realized I was not only an old blind man alone in the world, surrounded by darkness. I was a stupid old blind man alone in the world. Left to die by my own stupidity. My suffering made me see the stupidity of our traditions. My suffering became my teacher. Why do we have to kill each other? Why die for honor's sake when to live is to honor nature? All these questions haunted me as I stumbled over the forest, alone and blind.

I could no longer follow Tupi traditions that made me push my own son to his own death, for shame. So, I followed the paths in the forest open to the blind, the paths of sounds. I had heard of the community of Black men and women, but as I am blind I do not see color. I can only hear and sense a different people in you. When I found Palmares the people were kind to me. So kind, in fact, that I found myself a Black woman to be my eyes again. Zuleika taught me so much more than your language and the Portuguese language; she taught me kindness, forgiveness, and love. My son is dead forever, but then the gods gave me a wife and a daughter. How much this world can give you if only you stay alive to receive it."

***

Dreams and Nightmares of a Black Prince

At night Tuibae's story continues to haunt Zumbi: love, tradition, family, honor, death, all that are the stuff a prince is made of—and all this is now mixed with the Tupi traditions of war and death. Many a night since that day these themes come to visit him in dreams and in as many occasions as nightmares.

In dreams the Black folks, the Tupi people, and the Europeans live together in peace. Each group is devoted to raising their children and their crops. Their children are educated to love one another and allowed to fall in love with one another. The couples resulting from these random pickings of love are more and more mixed until one day there is a mass of humanity in which one cannot distinguish groups by color or creed. The dream brings a smile and relief and hope for the day to come and the years hidden in the future. Dreams unite.

Other nights these themes come as nightmares, as dives into fear and despair. The scourges of racism, bigotry, and prejudice continue to lash harder and harder at the backs of humankind. Whenever it disappears in one form it reemerges in another; as the Hydra fighting Hercules, each severed head gives rise to two new heads. In these nightmares Zumbi keeps on fighting as the beast grows and grows, finally biting his arm, sucking off his bones. As the nightmare continues the light dims in the sky, and a Portuguese snake starts to swallow its own tail, covering the sun. The snake seems to reduce itself more and more, as it continues to eat its own tail. The snake is humankind devouring itself and its hunger is slavery consuming itself until it engulfs everything, taking with it all hopes. In these nights Zumbi wakes up drenched in sweat and already weary of the day to come and of life in this world.

These are the dreams and nightmares of the sleeping hours, but there are also those of the waking hours, none more amazing and frightening than the dreams and nightmares of love.

***

Acirema

Acirema is then half Tupi, half African. Her eyes are green like the tropical trees that surround the quilombo while her hair falls over her shoulders pitch-black like the wings of the raven. Her skin color takes on a dark deep bronze no matter the season of the year.

Zumbi and Acirema fall into the infinite blessing of the first innocent love of children. They seem to seek each other every day, and those moments in which they are in each other's sight are enough to make such days complete. When they see each other, their hearts skip a beat together and their breathing takes a pause—and with that the world has a moment of peace. Their love does not know carnality; it belongs to the other dimensions of existence that only children know and adults have forgotten.

Each song by Wonder in the weekly banquets reminds Zumbi of Acirema, each vision of beauty sung through his music brings her image to mind. There is even a sad slow song Wonder sings that talks about solitude in the morning, when dust is coming down, that never fails to bring Zumbi visions of Acirema's face and the sound of her voice, even the scent of her presence. He knows then and there this song will always bring him those visions and sounds and scents—no matter when or where he is.

English Interlude: Cambridge, 1666

The Great Plague had reached Cambridge from London in 1665 and since then college classes had been dismissed. Ever since he was a small boy, he had a taste and talent for mechanics, building windmills, water clocks, kites, and sundials. Now as an adult he builds a reflective telescope.

His mind turns to the heavens, with a solid mathematical grip and geometry tools. Now he can see and observe the celestial bodies in motion. His mind needs to explain and measure the forces at play in the cosmic dance. The greatest of these forces will be tamed by his unquiet mind:

> *In the same year I began to think of gravity extending to the orb of the Moon ... compared the force requisite to keep the Moon in her orb with the force of gravity at the surface of the earth and found they answer pretty nearly.*

In 1668 he looks back at the years of the plague and all his accomplishments and concludes:

> *All this was in the two years of 1665 and 1666 for in those years I was in the prime of my age for invention and minded Mathematics and Philosophy more than at any time since.*

He is mistaken.

Back at Trinity College he is elected fellow and then Lucasian Professor of Mathematics.

It will take him almost twenty years to start making his work on gravity known and complete his magnus opus

Mathematical Principles of Natural Philosophy or, as published in Latin: *Philosophiae Naturalis Principia Mathematica.*

Near his death, in 1727, at the ripe age of eighty-seven, he will say:

> *I do not know what I may appear to the world, but to myself I seem to have been only like a boy playing on the seashore, and diverting myself in now and then finding a smoother pebble or a prettier shell than ordinary, whilst the great ocean of truth lay all undiscovered before me.*

His pebble and his shell are the moon and sun. His name is Isaac Newton.

CHAPTER 6

A TEST IN THE JUNGLE

Every education system needs tests to verify the learning of its students and attest to the teaching techniques of its masters. The combat and weapons classes are no different. Zumbi and his cohort of African boys and girls are learning to fight with swords and knives, bows and arrows, slings, and their own arms and legs using capoeira skills. Given their royal charges, Zumbi and Andala also learn and practice with some of the few muskets available at the quilombo. At the end of that year of training they have mastered the basics of their weapons of choice.

"You are now ready for a test on weapons," begins the Moor. "Learning Capoeira takes longer so you will need more training. As for weapons, this first test is quite simple. Each of you will leave at twilight to the forest with your sword, your bow, and five arrows. You can return when you bring back a wild animal. Dead."

Antonio Soares looks at Zumbi with a sparkle in his eyes.

"You know the trick for this one: go and kill a bird or a monkey. It's easy. Be back in time for dinner!"

Zumbi looks at the other boys as they rush to get their equipment and head to the forest. He stays behind with the Moor.

"Since you learned the musket, you may take it as well."

Zumbi looks at him with a serious gaze.

"I will not take my musket. That is not fair to the others. Nor will I kill a bird nor a monkey."

The Moor gives him a patient smile.

"So, what are you after, Prince Zumbi?"

"I will bring you the jaguar that is killing cattle around the Macaco. That is a fairer test for these skills."

"My prince, expeditions were sent against this beast and came back empty handed. King Ganga Zumba, your uncle, is organizing another group to go out in the next full moon."

"I am not afraid."

"Remember, my boy, the mighty lion in Africa kills by crushing the soft windpipe, and the jaguars of these lands crush their prey's bony spine. They do that with one powerful bite right where the skull meets the spinal cord. Instead of going for the soft throat, the jaguar goes for the hard bone, crushes it. The prey falls paralyzed right there, instantly."

"My arrows and sword can kill too."

"The jaguar is a killer of killers. Stay away from it."

The Brazilian jaguar is indeed the king of its tropical jungles and forests. Among the jaguar's prey are fish, birds, deer, armadillos, peccaries, porcupines, tapirs, capybaras, anacondas, and even caimans. When near cattle ranches, they attack calves and small cows. The jaguar prefers the deep forest but when humans start to move in, they move into the jaguar's territory. With the humans come cows, pigs, and chickens, only adding to the jaguar's vast lunching and dining options.

Way up north from Palmares there are legends about a river so full of jaguars in its margins that it is called Jaguaribe. One day the Portuguese will build in its proximity an enchanted town to be named Jaguaruana and in those northern distances one day slavery will start to decompose, taking with it the Brazilian empire. Those stories however, live still in the future.

In the present time, Black farmers near Macaco are losing calves to a jaguar that made the surrounding woods its dominion.

Several cows at those ranches now also carry the markings of the jaguar paw: four streaks of blood running down the neck. These are the lucky ones.

Zumbi enters the forest where the other students had but heads in a different direction. The livestock stays to the west so he walks around the perimeter of the village and looks for jaguar prints in the soft ground. While the other boys look up for birds, Zumbi looks down, examining the ground with eyes and hand. Before the first bird is taken down by an arrow, Zumbi finds the first paw prints on the clay. They lead him deep into the forest as the sunlight is disappearing from the sky.

The forest at night is pitch-black dark. What during the day is full of paths and ways, at night is a deep black hole out of which the fears of men, women, and beasts are born. The forest is also quiet at night, each animal seeking shelter from the night hunters, and only those hunters are fully alert and doing their work of killing.

The jaguar is the king of the Brazilian jungle and its roar announces the start of the hunt. In that sense it is the opposite of the rooster, who in the morning announces *I survived another night*. Thus, they affirm the existence of nocturnal

and diurnal animals, humans only occupying the hybrid cre-
puscular zone between night and day. Zumbi, as the African
prince of Palmares, moves carefully and quietly, leaving the
day and entering the night. He takes an arrow from his
quiver and keeps it ready in his bow, his hands holding the
tension. These same hands are now moving in synchrony
with his eyes. He looks right with eyes and hands, he looks
left with eyes and hands, he takes another step.

The night, at last, falls upon the mountains of Palmares.
Zumbi is so far from the village he only sees a few fires, the
last stars in the dark night. Now, the cold comes down and
takes hold and the forest goes to sleep. The stars of the Southern hemisphere pepper the sky, constellations illustrating the
dark canvas of the heavens. In this night, silence and cold
and darkness fall upon the forest and are Zumbi's only com-
panions. Until the jaguar announces his hunt.

The jaguar's roar is now Zumbi's guiding star in this
darkness. With his vision useless, he depends on his ears and
his nose only. He eventually even closes his eyes, which seems
to amplify his hearing. He holds his breath. A breaking
branch to the left and above makes him turn in one swift
move, letting the arrow out.

Zzzsh!

The first arrow flies silently through the night air and
hits a tree in the distance. A thump to the ground to his left
announces the jaguar is near and he sent the arrow in the
right direction.

With a shaking hand, Zumbi takes out another arrow and
readies it in the bow. His breath is fast, his hand steadies, his
heart pounces like a drum inside his chest. Nothing moves.
Another roar echoes through the trees. Now to the right,
ground level. Zumbi looks and sees nothing in the night.

"I have to see with my ears now."

Zzzsh!

The second arrow bounces into another tree. Again, in the move practiced so many times in class, his left hand pulls out another arrow and readies it in the bow. One deep breath at a time; the arrow should fly between heartbeats. The jaguar must be closer now. Behind him, a branch snap. He turns and lets another arrow go.

Zzzsh!

The third arrow keeps flying, meeting nothing for a long instant. The jaguar is circling him. He wants to find its speed, define its method. Again, to the right, leaves brush against spotted feline fur. He can sense the jaguar's location and then another roar confirms it.

Zzzsh!

The fourth arrow flies blind into the night. The jaguar jumps, sensing its power. Again, above ground level, flying light as a bird. A bird with a bite that can crush bones and destroy vertebrae. Ahead of him, on top of some tree. Right in front of him.

Zzzsh!

The fifth arrow flies up while the jaguar flies down. The arrow misses by a few inches, the jaguar does not. It lands it on top of Zumbi, pushing him back. He is surprised by its weight, its power, its muscles rock solid. He falls back. The jaguar retreats and opens its mouth. Even in this dark night Zumbi can see the four ivory canine teeth and smell its breath. One more roar echoes in the forest.

Everything now feels like slow motion, for a lot happens in a quick instant. Zumbi's right hand drops the bow and reaches to his sword. The jaguar's weight falls on top of him. He can barely breathe, let alone move. The bite, the most powerful of feline bites, is coming to his throat. He raises his elbow to protect his throat while his hand grabs his sword. As his elbow hits the jaguar's own throat he hits its face with the sword's pommel. The beast retreats in pain, not used to prey fighting back this hard. Zumbi stands up; the jaguar stares at him, ready to pounce again. With the sword in his right hand Zumbi moves like a capoeira master. The jaguar pounces but Zumbi rolls, sword up, transpiercing the animal as it comes down on him.

The jaguar gives one final roar—one sad and painful roar aimed at the dark skies. Zumbi breathes slowly under the many pounds of animal power and flesh. The jaguar is dead. He pushes it to the side.

Zumbi gathers some branches to help carry the body back to the village. Looking at the stars he can find his way back even in a moonless night. As he prepares to move out, another roar, this one faint, catches his ear. This is not an adult roar. Now examining the dead animal, he realizes it's a female jaguar.

The sound of the cub guides him to their nesting place. It is only one and Zumbi can barely see it. It is a little cub, deep black spots running all over the golden fur, bright eyes with a shadow of fear.

"Hey Little One. Come here."

The little cub takes time to move until it cautiously gets out of their hiding place and jumps. Zumbi catches him midair.

"I got your mama. She was killing my people's cattle."

The cub makes a nest now in Zumbi's arm muscles.

"I wish I had not done that. I had to. She was going to kill me too."

The cub stares at him, with deep yellow feline eyes.

"I will take care of you. I promise."

From that day on Zumbi and the jaguar become one. From a bloody encounter in the middle of a dark night begins a friendship of two orphans united in such a deep bond, even death would not set them apart. He calls her *Pintada* meaning painted spots in Portuguese.

The villagers are surprised when they see their prince coming back, dragging a huge dead jaguar and followed by its small cub. When they approach them, the cub runs to the protection of Zumbi's legs.

And thus, Zumbi finds his pet.

The Occult History of Brazil

The sun god Tupã and his sister, the moon goddess Arasy, descended in a hill in Paraguay and created the first man Rupave and the first woman Sypave. This first couple had three sons and thirty daughters. Their son Marangatú had a daughter named Kerana who was seduced by Tao, the spirit of evil. Together, Kerana and Tao birthed seven monsters.

The first is Teju Jagua whose body is covered with scales and walks on all fours. This first-born is a dragon that hides in caves and prefers darkness to the light. Those that dwell in the shadows and prefer to live in caves owe allegiance to Teju Jagua.

The second is Mbói Tu'I, who was born with the body of a snake and the head of a parrot. This son lives in waterways and protects the fish and other aquatic beasts. People living close to rivers and lakes, who feed on fish and oysters, sacrifice to Mboi Tu'I.

The third is Monai, the spirit of air and open fields, whose body is that of a serpent and whose head contains horns. Monai steals unattended people, animals, and objects, taking them to his cave. When you fail to pay attention to a person, or an animal, or an object, you leave them prey to Monai.

The fourth is Yasy Yatere, a short man with blond hair and blue eyes. He is the protector of daytime naps and captures those caught awake to feed to his younger brother Ao Ao.

The fifth is Kurupi whose member is so long it stands wrapped around his waist. He is the source of lust and desire. Young passionate couples with urges and carnality pay homage to Kurupi.

The sixth is Ao Ao who has a taste for human flesh captured by his older brother Yasy Yatere.

The seventh is Luison, a werewolf who feeds on rotten corpses and whose touch is a harbinger of death.

It is in this commonwealth of werewolves, cannibals, and chimeras that the Portuguese will land and out-monster them by introducing slavery.

CHAPTER 7

THE ATTACK OF 1667

"Five hundred Portuguese troops!"

That is the terse report from the night watch. King Ganga Zumba looks at the shaken young soldier and sends a group of more experienced officers to the location. The group returns after counting eight standards in the advanced detachment followed by sixteen in the bulk contingent. The king sends for all his advisors.

"Tell Zumbi and Andala to come here too."

By midday all the advisors and commanders from each village are together at the royal compound in Macaco for an emergency meeting. The returning officers confirm the first report, only adding a note of dread.

"This is a Portuguese regiment. They come for us, all of us. I am not losing men like we did to the Black captain"— he never pronounces the name —"We are going to fight, and they are going to die or go back to Recife."

The silence in the room is a collective agreement. There is only resolution in each commander's face. At twelve years of age, Zumbi and Andala are the youngest among these men who by now are used to their presence, as well as to that of the jaguar Pintada, who lies down and seems to nap undisturbed by the anxiety floating in the room. Master Yalom makes his calculations about the manpower and timeline for each detachment.

"The advanced party has about one hundred and fifty men followed by the bulk of the troops two days behind, about three hundred and fifty men."

The Moor, usually quiet, speaks on military considerations and battle prospects.

"We can match them in manpower but not in weapons capacity. Each Portuguese has his own musket. We have one for each ten or twenty men. With these many muskets, their direct firepower will be overwhelming. It will cost us to stop them."

The room is quiet for a long time.

"We can move west," says one.

"Remember the Tupi people—they will not give away their land. And to have us fighting the natives is the Portuguese's greatest dream," replies another.

The king closes that discussion. "We will not run anymore and we will not engage the Tupi. They have been friends to us."

Silence returns to the room.

"We could use Cesar's strategy in the battle of Alesia," Zumbi's voice speaks from the back.

All eyes in the room move to the young prince. He steps forward and takes a place among the military advisors.

"We start with their advanced troops, their vanguard, and surround them with a circumvallation that will prevent them getting reinforcements, ammunition, or provisions. It is a smaller group, so our men can build that perimeter in the dead of night and they will awake encircled. The tall fence will eliminate their advantage with the muskets," Zumbi says.

"But then their full contingent will get to us in two days," counters someone. "We will be unprotected from their shots, and that is when their bigger firepower will make a difference. We have no way to defend from their musket fire on the ground. We will be crushed in the fence we build ourselves."

Zumbi does not miss a beat.

"That is why we then have two days to build an outside fence, this time protecting us. A contravallation. Each palisade will have raised platforms from which we can shoot arrows and slings down without being hit by their muskets from the ground."

Another heavy silence falls on the room. Each advisor ponders the unusual strategy quietly. So unusual it might even work. They all know the deadly challenge posed by the efficiency of Portuguese muskets: they can fire from such a distance no arrow can get to them. The Portuguese make a firing wall that pierces everything in sight. These firing lines can quickly decimate a group of African warriors armed with swords, arrows. and spears. If only they could fly.

King Ganga Zumba breaks the silence.

"The prince is correct. These fences will give us the advantage of hitting them from above while protecting our men from their shots from below."

Silence returns, now signaling agreement with a hint of hope. Now they have plan of action.

The next nights and days are spent preparing, planning, and practicing building fences and fortifications. All that can be heard across the five villages are the sounds of hammers hitting anvils, forging axes, shovels, swords, and arrowheads. There is a natural rhythm to each bantu craftsman and, working in concert, their tools' sounds spread an energy that seems to sparkle in each villagers' eye. The busy blacksmiths also prepare a new special weapon designed by Master Ya-lom: whistling sling bullets. These bullets are shot from slings and weigh about one ounce each with a tiny hole that makes them soar in the air as they fly toward their target. Because Zumbi is particularly good at throwing these sling bullets and the king asks him to lead a squadron of their best slingers, an addition to the fence-and-arrow strategy.

After a report comes that the advancing party is encamped just a few miles from Amaro, Ganga Zumba gives the order to move the troops. The men and women of the African army hug their spouses and kiss their children. There is not much time for long goodbyes and the people of Palmares are by now used to fighting for their freedom to exist as a free people—constantly. Even the girls and boys want to follow and fight with their parents at the front.

The Palmares troops know the forest well and get to their location by nightfall. They now can see where the Portuguese camp is and their engineers calculate where the fence needs to go up. They need a bigger circle to make sure the sounds of building it do not alert the slumbering troops or their watchers.

All night the forest is alive with whispers and murmurs of an army moving logs and slowly and stealthily putting the tall fence together. Their murmurs are also muffled by the orchestra of mosquitos, crickets, cicadas, and night owls that comes to perform every night in these tragic tropics.

As the day breaks, and the sun pushes the light into the morning, the Portuguese find themselves surrounded by a tall fence on all sides. There is not much they can do besides try to get out, and at the first sight of one man attempting to break through the fence an arrow flies down, transpiercing his arm and leaving him screaming on the ground. Now fear spreads over the Portuguese, brought by the slow understanding that they are trapped. Their only hope now is the arrival of reinforcements they know are two days away.

Realizing they will just lose men by fighting a wall where arrows come flying from above, they decide to lie low and wait, biding their time. They have more than two days' worth of rations and they can afford to wait for their own commanders and comrades.

Meanwhile, the Black troops work diligently on the outer fence: the same height, the same platform for bowmen. Ganga Zumba and the princes oversee all construction, while the Moor ensures the troops' readiness. The men smile at the young princes but their commanding attitude quickly gets them serious and back to work.

Two days later, the outer fence is ready to welcome the Portuguese rearguard. Stumbling upon this fence in the woods, the Portuguese do not hesitate to attack. Hearing the musket fire from outside, the men on the inside also mount an attack of their own. The arrows fly down non-stop, both inside and outside. The Black soldiers are prepared for this double attack. Furthermore, Ganga Zumba has one final surprise: another squadron is waiting to surprise the Portuguese troops from outside and make them feel surrounded—which they are.

Zumbi moves with his small slingers detachment to wherever the action is. As they come in, each man hurls multiple bullets with each throw. The sound of these whistling bullets quickly becomes a signal for the Portuguese to run away. The screaming flying menaces get the Portuguese morale down quickly.

A day follows of multiple advances toward the fences both outside and inside with no breach. One Black soldier is killed by a musket shot, all other shots hitting the fence. In the same day several Portuguese troops are killed or injured by arrows and sling bullets. The Portuguese commander also knows his inside troops will run out of ammunition soon.

"Can this be the fate of five hundred Portuguese troops?" the frustrated Portuguese commander asks his aides "We fought the Dutch and now will be defeated by a band of runaway slaves?" Their answer is silence and this silence speaks volumes.

Night falls. The troops are quiet. Ganga Zumba orders torches of the double fences. The sight of fire floating above the treetops gives the Portuguese a sense of foreboding they cannot control. The men on the inside are even more fearful. Without ammunition, which is running low, they will be slaughtered by the Palmares troops with arrows and even with swords and axes.

The morning comes. The Portuguese commander brings his advisors to his tent.

"We need to settle and get the hell out of here."

"And go back to Recife defeated by Black men?" one lieutenant asks, indignant.

The commander smiles bitterly.

"In case you have not noticed, that is what just happened. We have just been defeated by Black men. That is the plain and painful truth. At least we are still alive to tell this tale."

"We are still here! We can fight them!"

"Have you seen this dammed fence? Can you imagine what your comrades are feeling inside that trap right now? Trapped by these same Black men! Sitting ducks to their slings and arrows!"

The advisors fall silent. Even the indignant lieutenant is quiet now. Nobody wants to look their commander in the eye.

"I will go and settle this. I want my men back. And I want them back alive."

The commander gets out and orders a standard bearer to come with him. The baffled pair approaches the fence.

"I come in peace! I want to negotiate with your leader!"

On the platform the message is passed quickly all the way to Ganga Zumba.

"I will go," says Zumbi.

Ganga Zumba responds.

"No. They will come to us."

The king's serenity surprises his advisors and he continues.

"Tell their commander I will see him inside our perimeter. And make sure you use that word."

The royal response reaches the Portuguese camp and the commander does not want to go in. Night falls again.

Next morning, they try another attack. Musket fire from outside and inside again. This time no Black warrior is hurt as they learn how to best use the fence protection and several more Portuguese men fall prey to the raining arrows and sling bullets. From that attack there is an incident that lingers in the memory of just two individuals: Zumbi and Ganga Zumba.

In the middle of the barrage of musket fire one Portuguese troop takes direct aim at the king's chest. Zumbi is the one who notices it and at the last moment before the soldier pulls the trigger hits the man's face with a precise whistling sling bullet. The musket falls to the ground, firing at nothing; the man falls to the other side with his hand holding his bloody face. Zumbi opens his generous smile and beams at the king. Ganga Zumba nods seriously, says nothing, and moves on commanding his lancers' maneuvers.

By afternoon the Portuguese commander is ready to capitulate again and now agrees to come inside the perimeter. Once inside Ganga Zumba receives him surrounded by his advisors, Zumbi and Andala by his sides.

"Speak."

"I want to take my men back. We will leave."

"You come to my land, with armed men, and just want to leave?"

"We just wanted to capture some slaves back. These are property—"

Ganga Zumbi raises his hand. The Portuguese commander stops speaking at once.

"These are not property. These are men and women. These are not slaves. These are enslaved people. Nobody is a slave. People are enslaved. They are fathers and mothers who have children. Like you."

The Portuguese is quiet, listening to all without a word, his eyes staring at the ground. Hate seems to emanate from his pores. King Ganga Zumba proceeds:

"You can leave as long as you surrender all muskets. You brought those weapons to our land; they are confiscated now. They belong to us now."

"How do you guarantee their safe departures, if they are unarmed?"

"You have my word. That will suffice."

The Portuguese's eyes grow wide with a mix of surprise, anger, and fear. It takes him a long time to respond. Ganga Zumba is patient, beaming at Andala.

"You can have them, damn it. But I want all my men out. They will leave their muskets behind as they go."

And so it is done: the Portuguese depart, defeated, deflated, and disarmed. The word of Ganga Zumba to let them leave untouched is strictly followed by each Black man. The men and women from Palmares are now ready to return and celebrate their greatest victory and the greatest increase in their arsenal for freedom.

Before they leave this camp of double fences, which will now belong to the legends of Palmares, they have one task: they will bury here the one Black soldier killed in action.

As they prepare the ground for their fallen comrade the Palmares men notice the several crosses marking the burial grounds of the Portuguese. Zumbi cries as they lower the body into the grave, thinking about the man's children and wife. He asks Ganga Zumba:

"Uncle, our friend died just like the Portuguese men did. In the end it is all the same."

"Yes, Zumbi. We all start the same and end the same. The king of Portugal and the poorest person are born both in warm blood and pain. The king of Portugal and the poorest person die and turn cold in a day."

"Then, are we all the same? Enslaved and enslaving?"

"The difference lies in what happens between birth and death. That is a difference that makes a difference. That is our opportunity to choose: spend your days fighting for the freedom of your people or spend your nights fighting to imprison the children of other mothers."

"Yes, uncle. What I am afraid is that as long we as we keep doing the work of death, we will never be on the side of life. We are good at it. We are good at killing. Maybe it is part of our nature."

Ganga Zumbi hears without arguing the points made by his young nephew.

From that day on, those grounds and those crosses mark an important event for Palmares: the day young Prince Zumbi used a strategy of the greatest of Romans to defeat a superior force. At age twelve his fame starts to spread across the villages of the quilombo, bringing pride to Palmares and concern to Recife.

***

In the village of Zambi the fierce Dandara, seven years old, hears, enchanted, the stories of the Battle of the Two Fences, and of Prince Zumbi, told by Chief Chiamaka, her father.

The Occult History of Portugal

1119

Hugues de Payns and Geoffrey de Saint-Omer, two French knights, meet in Jerusalem, where the Temple of Solomon once stood, and promise to devote their lives to defending pilgrims to the Holy Land. In the year of our Lord they create a monastic order eventually named as the Order of the Knights of the Temple. The order will become immensely wealthy and enter history with the name of Templars. They create the first international banking network and challenge the power of kings and at times the Pope himself. They wear a white robe with a red cross.

1307

The king of France owns the Templars money and favors. The order holds land and property throughout Paris and all over the countryside. Their headquarters would become in due time the Bastille. The king's troops arrest the warrior monks in one October night; many are beheaded on the spot. Two processes are open against the order: one by the King of France, the second by the Pope in Rome. Both are eager to have their hands in the order's treasure.

1314

The processes against the order are finalized. Three Templar leaders are to be burned at the stake in Paris, one of them the Grand Master Jacques Molay, now approaching seventy years of age. Out of the flames his voice is heard through the crowd thus cursing the French king and the Pope:

"King Phillip and Pope Clement! I, Jacques de Molay, Grand Master of the Templar order, summon you to the tribunal of God in heaven. I will see you soon!"

> *S'en vendra en brief temps meschie* / *Let evil swiftly befall*
> *Sus celz qui nous dampnent a tort;* / *Those who have wrongly condemned us;*
> *Diex en vengera nostre mort.* / *God will avenge our death.*

Before the year is over both the king and the Pope are dead.

One final mystery remains: what happened to the Templars' treasure? When the accounting is finalized, the riches are not even close to what was imagined by the king or the Pope.

The order is now extinguished in all kingdoms of Europe except one: Portugal.

In the following two centuries this small Iberian kingdom embarks on navigations never before dreamed of, discovering new worlds and connecting the globe for the first time by the ocean. The Portuguese caravels sail between the new and the old world, displaying huge white sails bearing deep red crosses.

The eternal knights' temple still stands among the magnificent Portuguese hills in the enchanted city of Tomar.

CHAPTER 8

INITIATION

1668

Doriana, royal advisor to King Ganga Zumba and master of the trivium, is still married to the most mysterious man to live in the quilombo: Hermes Seixas.

Now, almost five years after his arrival, and a year after the victory of 1667, Hermes asks again for an audience with the king and royal cabinet. Hermes is ready to initiate someone in the Mysteries and he wants the king to authorize his ceremony. This is something Hermes has been preparing for since he got to Palmares.

The king asks him to point to the person to be initiated. Many believe the king himself will be the one chosen to dive into the mysteries of magic. Some believe it will be Doriana. Everyone in the room watches in quiet anticipation. The silence is deep, as if the room is holding its breath.

Hermes has his tall staff and he goes around the room, looking each person in the eye. Eventually he finds his way to the center of the large hall. His voice is calm and deep but the words are in a language nobody understands anymore; to speak with the old gods one needs African words now forgotten.

Naomba mungu wa Afrika anielekeze kwa mteule!

Finally, he raises his staff again and moves it around the room like the hand of a gigantic clock. When he stops all eyes move toward the person pointed out by the long staff held out by the old man's arm. All eyes are on the thirteen-year-old prince Zumbi.

Ganga Zumba regains command of the room and celebrates the selection. All around the room there is relief mixed with envy. The other thirteen-year-old prince, Andala, leaves the room. Thirteen is the magical age when the Jewish people recognize one coming to be accountable for his action with the bar mitzvah, when the Catholics call for the seven steps of confirmation.

Hermes takes Zumbi by the hand and they walk outside alone.

"We are going to spend the night outside and inside. Or inside and outside."

Pintada follows them, all the while keeping an eye on Hermes walking by Zumbi. The trio disappears into the forest.

The walk proceeds in silence until they find themselves following a small stream descending from a pond formed by a waterfall. When they stop at the water's edge, Hermes looks at Zumbi then at Pintada. The lush green of the tropical forest is the frame around them and the waterfall that feeds the pond.

"Where I am taking you, you should come alone and only bring all your ancestors in your heart."

Hermes looks at Pintada who looks disappointed at the dark waters of the pond. Zumbi tells him:

"She will wait here, if we are going into the water."

"We are going into the water and then we are going on a land inside the land," Hermes says. "You follow me."

Hermes walks into the pond, slowly disappearing into the water. Zumbi follows him quickly before he can lose sight of his elder.

Underwater Zumbi can see Hermes swiftly moving and he pushes himself hard. The water is dark and all he sees is the man ahead of him, his feet mostly visible. Time seems to stretch and the lungs start to beg for air, the need to breathe spreading from his chest to the whole body. Zumbi looks and the movement of the water tells him they are swimming now under the waterfall. Through the water he sees Hermes moving in front of him, his only guide in this underwater world.

His lungs are close to exploding and now going back may take longer than going forward. Zumbi swims ahead. It takes all his self-control to prevent him from swimming up to try to find air.

Finally, a faint light appears ahead and Hermes cannot be seen in the water anymore. Zumbi uses his last strength to emerge in a small cave where darkness is only broken by a few rays of light coming through holes in the stone ceiling. The fingers of light spread a fading glow.

The young prince spends a few minutes catching his breath. The air is cold and almost refreshing in this hidden cave. As he emerges, he sees other sources of light: seven black candles surrounding Hermes, who is now sitting cross-legged on the floor. By him, hanging from the ceiling by its hind legs is a lamb, bleating wildly.

Hermes gestures to Zumbi, pointing to a sitting mat right in front of him. Zumbi sits. The bleating continues, now louder since he is sitting by the lamb. Hermes pulls out a knife and with one swift movement cuts the lamb's throat. The bleating stops; the bleeding begins.

"You are in the cave and you have always been in the cave."

Zumbi nods.

"You know the allegory of the cave?" Hermes asks.

"Yes, we studied it at the trivium class."

"Tell me about it."

"Plato uses it to illustrate how our perceptions can deceive us. A group of people is tied in a cave all their lives and there is a fire behind them. All they can see are the shadows on the wall and they believe all they see there is all there is. Some free themselves from the chains and finally understand all they were looking at are shadows. Those who are still tied think they have lost their minds."

"You are a good student, as my wife told me many times. The proof is your answer is complete, informed, and absolutely wrong."

Zumbi is taken aback for a moment but continues the conversation with the short strange man in front of him.

"How so?"

"The cave we are all born tied to is the bony envelop of the skull. We live inside our heads and need to get out to see beyond the shadows projected in its walls. And yes, those who do will be called insane. Yet to be wise, you will need to expand your mind beyond the enclosed walls of your skull."

The lamb's blood drips from the throat to the ground, from there flowing slowly and warmly toward the water. It touches Zumbi's sitting leg and he feels its warmth. Zumbi's eyes are now wide open. Hermes continues:

"The lips of wisdom are closed, except to the ears of understanding."

Zumbi nods, saying nothing. Hermes hands him a cup full of milk which he drinks in one take.

"Milk quiets the thirst and the hunger. It is a sacred drink that mixes the vegetable the cattle eats in the animal body and brings forward its power, strength, and energy. The world starts in the mineral realm and from it life emerges. Life builds structures out of minerals. First, life was in the vegetable beings, then migrated to the animal bodies. Humans can combine the mineral, the vegetable, and the animal in one body. Now that your body is satisfied, we need to satisfy the thirst and the hunger in your soul for knowledge and wisdom."

***

Seven Principles

"There are the seven principles that will create all knowledge available to people in all places and at all times. Each principle contains secrets within it and several wise men and women have spent their lives studying just one of them. Here I will give you all of them. Then you will spend the rest of your life developing your own understanding of these seeds. Are you ready?"

Zumbi just looks and nods at Hermes, who continues in the same quiet tone.

"The first principle is that of mentalism: first came mind, then came matter. The pale hand believes matter creates mind. We know it is the other way around: mind creates matter. In the beginning there was a word. And the word was love. God was love. God is love. The word first became mineral, then plant, and animal, then men and women. These forms still fight today, mineral against plant, plant against animal, animal against men and women. At the same time the plants feed on minerals, the animals feed on plants, and men and women feed on animals and on plants and on minerals. All because we come from the mind, we are all mind."

One candle goes out.

"The second principle is of correspondence: on earth as it is in heaven. There is always a correspondence across the dimensions of being. The law applies to all, up and down, high and low. Understanding of the law in one dimension will follow into another. There are infinite dimensions, yet all follow these laws, which are universal. Take these principles with you wherever you go, day or night, North or South, in life and in death. They will follow."

A second candle goes out.

"The third principle is that of vibration: nothing is resting, everything is moving, all the world vibrates. All things are but strings. The universe is pulsating, beaming with energy and life. If you develop your deep hearing you will hear the music of the celestial spheres. One who can harness that energy can move mountains."

A third candle goes out.

"The fourth principle is that of polarity: everything is dual, all have their opposite. Day and night. Black and white. Sound and silence. Love and hate. Land and water. Fire and air. Men and women. North and south. East and west. Life and death. Good and evil. Sun and Moon. All things are double, one against the other."

The fourth candle goes out.

"The fifth principle is that of rhythm. The pendulum compensates the opposites and moves the world, all in its proper time. The movement in one direction feeds the next move opposing it. In your heart, one beat pushes the blood; the other pulls the blood. You breathe in and you breathe out. You sleep to wake up, you wake up to sleep."

The fifth candle goes out. Darkness grows.

"The sixth principle is that of causation. For every cause, there is an effect; for every effect there is a cause. Everything that occurs, occurs within the law, and chance is the product of a law we do not recognize. It is the few who know the things that they see are only effects and who can then understand the causes by which these effects were brought into existence. When the thought has been trained to look below the surface, everything takes on a different appearance."

The sixth candle goes out, leaving one single source of light.

"The seventh principle is that of gender. In all things there is a masculine and a feminine. Gender is organizing the world between these two ways of being. And one exists inside the other. When you see one, look for the other because that other is looking also."

The seventh candle goes out and now they are alone in the darkness that engulfs them. Without seeing Hermes' calm face, Zumbi only hears his voice at this moment.

"Repeat with me: mentalism, correspondence, vibration, polarity, rhythm, causation, and gender. Each day of the week you devote to remind yourself of one of these principles. Monday, Tuesday, Wednesday, Thursday, Friday, Saturday, and Sunday were built to follow these principles. They organize our time; they organize our mind. That is why we have seven days in the week. And every new week you start all over again."

A gush of air moves inside the cave and a small firepit lights up in front of Zumbi. Hermes is gone. There is a plate of grilled meat for him and a jar of water.

Zumbi eats, then sleeps, and dreams, alone in the cave.

Next morning, he walks back to the Macaco and all along the way he feels different. Even Pintada at first fails to recognize him. People see their prince and also see in him something changed; something different moves in his eyes and his body. There is confidence but there is also a deep sadness, the sadness of understanding the universe more to-day than yesterday. The sadness of knowing there is no return in learning about the deep layers of being.

Hermes welcomes him back with an embrace and as he does, he whispers in Zumbi's ear:

"Yesterday we saw the boy leave the community, today we welcome the man back. They boy died so the man could be born. Your body is now shielded. No weapons carried by pale hands will ever reach you."

These words surprise Zumbi, for he had heard about the shielded body but he thought it was just a legend. He looks at this forearms and hands; they look the same. The palms of his hands are still marked by the lines of destiny. From now on the rest of his whole body is marked by the lines of mystery.

Austrian Interlude: Vienna, 1668

The opera is so complex it takes him an extra couple of years of work, so instead of celebrating the imperial wedding it will celebrate the Empress Margaret Theresa's seventeenth birthday. The piece is so long it will have to be performed over two days in a specially designed open-air theater in Vienna. The stagecraft includes shipwrecks and collapsing columns to tell the story of the golden apple of discord.

That story, also known as the Judgement of Paris, is the trigger for the oldest of stories: the Trojan War. It starts when the goddess of discord, Eris, is snubbed in a wedding and decides to throw a golden apple into the festivities with the inscription *to the fairest*. Three goddesses claim the prize: Aphrodite, Hera, and Athena. Zeus, not wanting to be the judge of such delicate matter, nominates the Trojan prince Paris, a mortal, to decide.

Paris observes them but cannot make up his mind. He then asks to see them in the nude to judge their total beauty undisturbed by clothing. They comply and he is given the privilege men seek through the ages. The goddesses proceed to attempt to bribe him: Hera with power over kingdoms, Athena with wisdom and knowledge, and Aphrodite with the love of the most beautiful mortal, Helen of Sparta, soon to be known for all time as Helen of Troy.

Paris does not hesitate and, as men are bound to, chooses love and lust over power or wisdom. Bought by the prospect of having Helen, Paris picks Aphrodite and thus incurs the ire of Hera and Athena. The merits and meaning of the ensuing war are to be discussed to the end of humanity's lifetime on planet Earth.

At the end of the opera performance in Vienna, the golden apple is thrown in turn to the young Austrian empress, herself a Spanish princess.

It is the climax of a life dedicated to music, first as a tenor, then as an organist, and finally now as a composer of operas and chamber cantatas. That career has taken him from his birthplace of Arezzo in Italy, to Venice, and then to Austria, first in Innsbruck and finally in the imperial capital of Vienna, a city that to this day is synonymous with opera.

He will die the following year, at the age of forty-six, as "the most celebrated Italian musician of his generation." His name is Pietro Antonio Cesti.

CHAPTER 9

THE BATTLE OF GARANHUNS

1670

To conquer the world, you must first conquer your own fear. That is the lesson the Greek Plutarch offers us in the story of Alexander and Bucephalus, told many centuries before Jesus walked the sands of Judea.

A horse trader from Thessaly, in northern Greece, brings a magnificent horse to show Philip, the king of Macedonia. The stallion comes with a pitch-black coat with a single mark, right in his forehead, of a star. All in court are in awe of such a beast until they try to mount it. The horse is wild and unmanageable, kicking high even at the sound of voices nearby. The king sends the trader and the horse away as useless. Alexander remarks "what an excellent horse they lose for not having the courage to approach and tame it." The king tries to ignore his son's remarks. Alexander repeats it a few times, to everyone's face. The king warns the young prince, still in his teens, "you speak to your elders as if you know more and could manage what they cannot?" The court silences except for Alexander, who answers calmly:

"I can tame that horse better than others."

"And if you fail?"

"I will pay the price in full."

The court now laughs while the king and his son settle the wager.

Alexander approaches Bucephalus and takes hold of the bridle, pulling the horse to face the sun. He has just realized the horse's own shadow was scaring him. Thus, we still say *he was afraid of his own shadow.* Alexander continues to hold the reins and let the horse at ease for a moment. He approaches and whispers in the horse's ears while gently stroking its crest and back. As the horse gets again agitated Alexander in one nimble leap mounts the horse, little by little drawing in the bridle—no spur and no striking. The horse is now impatient for a run and Alexander addresses him now with a commanding voice. They speed away, leaving the royal audience in suspense. They run and run, Alexander now a centaur on this huge black horse. They finally come back rejoicing and triumphing for the audience, which has burst into acclamations and applause. The king sheds tears: some say of joy, some say of relief. He embraces his son tight and whispers to him:

"Oh son! You must find a kingdom worthy of you, for Macedonia is too small!"

***

The First Graduating Test

At fifteen Zumbi is already a war veteran. After five years of training in the trivium, the quadrivium, and weapons and combat, it is time for the class to demonstrate all they have learned. The first graduating test is done as a collective test, when the whole class will be tested together.

As the only ones training in all disciplines, princes Zumbi and Andala are the natural leaders for this joint examination as it is a test of collective coordinated actions and skills.

All youth in training those five years is reunited and now for the first time the trivium and quadrivium groups meet to work together. Their teachers gather, Doriana leading the charge, sided by Master Yalom at one side, and the Moor at the other.

"To conquer in life, one must be unafraid to tame the wildest beast. And the wildest beast we will ever face is our own fear," she starts addressing all in attendance.

"To face our own fear, we need to know we can rely on each other. This is your joint and only test done as a group. You will succeed together or you will fail together. All must stand for one, and one for all. You must plan and execute the rescue of an enslaved family from one of the Portuguese plantations outside of Palmares. Before you go, our Christian chaplain will give you a special blessing."

The Palmares priest comes in front of the group with the usual Catholic salutations. He then orders them to kneel for the blessing that they will repeat in turn: the prayer of Saint George.

> *I will go dressed and armed with the weapons of Saint George*
> *so that my enemies, having feet will not reach me;*
> *having hands will not trap me;*
> *having eyes will not see me,*
> *neither with thought can they cause me harm.*
> *Firearms will not reach my body;*

knives and swords will break without touching my
body,
ropes and chains will break without tying my body.
Jesus Christ protects and defends me with the power
of His Holy and Divine Grace.
The Virgin of Nazareth covers me with her sacred
and divine mantle,
protecting me in all my dolors and afflictions.
And God, with His Divine Mercy and great power,
is my defender against the evils and persecutions of
my enemies.
Glorious Saint George, in the name of God,
extend to me your shield and your powerful arms,
defending me with your strength and your greatness;
and may my enemies underneath your feet become
humble and submissive to you.
So Be it in the Power of God, of Jesus Christ and of
the Divine Holy Spirit.
Amen

The community responds in unison: Amen.

The youth group had heard rumors about the joint test, but this is the first time they hear it spelled out clearly and to their own ears. They also know the simple solution is to organize an expedition to a plantation nearby Palmares and gather as many of those enslaved as possible. Most times these expeditions are done overnight, with silence and good coordination. Nobody gets lost, no shot is fired, they come back and are celebrated with the new African family they bring along.

Not this time.

Princes Zumbi and Andala gather with their teams at the edge of the village of Macaco. The parents look with apprehension to their growing teens, and they know they cannot interfere. It is time for their children to show they are full citizens of Palmares. Ready to defend, and if needed, to attack.

Andala wants to attack a new farm toward Porto Calvo in the east. Zumbi proposes a different approach.

"We are going to attack Garanhuns."

The newly formed village of Garanhuns, having evolved from a roadhouse to a town and then into a village in the span of a generation, is the largest prize on the way north; only one hundred and forty miles separate it from the provincial capital of Recife. Despite the precarious Portuguese roads, that distance can be easily covered in a two-day march. A proud village with cattle farms, sugar plantations, a small church, and some commerce, it is planted on top of a mountain with vast views of the forests surrounding it. And when you see the forest, the many eyes of the forest see you just as well.

The Portuguese forces always encamp for the rainy season. Their heavy weapons do not move quick in wet sand, their weight soaking deep in shifting roads and worse in mud. The Palmares troops are leaner, faster, and do not dread the waters, neither from above nor from below. For them, the mud can even be used to camouflage and ambush.

Most Portuguese regiments are settled in Recife at this time of the year. A few battalions are spread across villages in the hinterlands. In these villages farmers and plantation owners fend for themselves, usually with more brute force and less military discipline than regular troops.

The students, led by Andala, react with fearful skepticism to Zumbi's bold proposal.

"That village is too big a target for a practice!" says one.

Zumbi listens with attention to each argument as they continue to roll.

"They say we should not attack villages with churches that have more than one bell tower!" says another.

"We are going to get lost!" says a third.

"Worse yet, we are going to get caught, and sold—or executed!" says a fourth.

Finally, Zumbi raises his hand and they all stop talking.

"We can do it."

"But how?"

Zumbi points at the sky.

"See those rain clouds? They push the main Portuguese forces to the coast. They are now cowering in Recife at their headquarters. They do not stay in the backlands for the rainy season. Now look at us! The sling group can make rocks rain over them. Our archers can bring them death from a distance, silently. The infantry can take on any pale hand. Together, we can vanquish the small band of Portuguese troops that will be protecting a village like Garanhuns. With you and Pintada on my side I fear nothing."

At hearing her name Pintada roars as if in agreement, which serves to break the ice for the students.

Antonio Soares is the first to speak in support of the idea.

"We can do it, with our prince, we can do it." Then he repeats himself, but saying "with our *princes*."

Slowly the confidence spreads throughout the teen group. Sensing the tide turning, Andala keeps quiet.

"We can do it! We can do it!" repeats the group.

"Yes, we can," says Zumbi.

Zumbi gathers the leaders of the different teams, slings and arrows on one side, swords and knives on the other. The other students are told to prepare their gear and check their rations.

"We will travel as three teams through the forest. I take the slings, Antonio Soares the archers, and Andala and Yakini the swordsmen. We move quicker and safer this way. We meet every night to save on night watch duty. As we approach the village, we will need scouts. It is dangerous work."

And so they go.

They travel north and west guided by the stars and a few landmarks. The first night their anxiety is still palpable, but with each night it gets better. The scouts go ahead of the groups. On the fourth night they start to see signs of human occupation.

One scout returns with a prized finding: a slave from one of the Garanhuns farms. The slave is shaken with fear and dread. He has never seen a freed Black person before, let alone a troop of armed Black teens. He is brought directly to Zumbi.

"Kneel!" someone shouts from the back.

The poor soul throws himself to the ground, dividing his fearful stare between Zumbi and Pintada, who is sitting beside the prince.

"Spare me, Sir!"

"Stand up! You are a man and you are talking to men like you. Free men and women of Palmares."

The man stands up and looks at Zumbi.

"Are you prince Zumbi? They say you are only a legend, a made-up story. They say you are immortal."

Zumbi eases his commanding voice and asks with a smile, "When we have time, you can tell me about these tales about me. Now I need information about the village of Garanhuns."

The man is still bewildered and he looks around to the others whose eyes are fixed on Zumbi.

"What do you want to know?"

"When do they go to mass, when do they have their farmer's market, how many troops are stationed. That will be a good start."

The man takes his time, his eyes still lingering on the weapons carried by the troops.

"Mass is only on Sunday mornings because the priest is moving from villa to villa. The farmers and traders gather also on Sunday when everyone is in town."

"And the troops?"

"There is a sergeant and a few soldiers."

"How many is a few?"

"About six?"

"I want you to sit down with the engineers and draw as good a map of the town and the plantations surrounding it as your memory can produce."

"Yes, sir. Yes, sir."

The smile passes on Zumbi's face, which fades back to pensive.

***

The next day they can see the church towers. Now they wait for Sunday.

Sunday starts in Garanhuns with bells announcing the morning prayers. At the top of each hour they ring again. From each ranch, farm, and plantation there is movement toward the city center. Except for the enslaved who stay behind. They are not allowed to worship at the same church.

In each farm those enslaved Christians pray under the watchful eye of their foremen. Zumbi instructs the group leaders.

"We are attacking from the eight directions. The teams will mix now, each with a swordsperson and an archer. I will keep all the slings with me. Each team will be taking all farms and houses on the way to the city center. We cannot leave anyone behind to attack us from the rear. We move into the city center and we gather at the square before the mass is over. We have two hours to make it to the square. On approaching, stay down until we give the signal."

"What is the signal?"

"Slingshots at the church bell," Zumbi says with a playful look.

At each farm a detachment moves in quickly and approaches the foreman. If he touches his musket to react, the archer, man or woman, gets him down silently and quickly. Most surrender, so they move in, tie him up, and free the enslaved, and the group grows at a fast pace.

The action is now fast as Zumbi follows the history lesson drilled into him in the trivium classes: "careful planning and rapid execution." Resistance is met with no negotiation. Arrows fly at the first sign of danger. Foremen who resist die quickly while the majority just throw their hands in the air and are tied up. Only one fires his musket, which echoes through the mountains, and he is promptly killed by a silent arrow. At the sound of that musket, the Portuguese troops stationed at the city center look at each other and await orders from the sergeant, who is now attending mass. They are not interested in taking action without orders: one of the classic limitations of military training, discipline, and hierarchy.

As they move Zumbi has one preoccupation always in his mind: the supply of arrows.

On one farm two foremen are watching the enslaved. The team asks for reinforcements and waits. An extra archer comes in and two arrows fly parallel, leaving both foremen dead.

Most enslaved welcome the African teens, as they have heard stories about Palmares. A few slaves resist and want to stay in the security of bondage. Zumbi looks at them with deep sadness. They remind him of an old jaguar who lost the will to fight and survive.

As they approach the Portuguese headquarters at the city center, Zumbi reconvenes his troops and plans the final attack. He wants to give them a chance to surrender before engaging the Portuguese soldiers. He changes plans.

"Let us attack the church first."

They move on, guided by the sight of the bell towers.

"Bring the slings."

The slings arrive and Zumbi himself gets his own sling out.

"We are going to hit the bells. I want to get them out, scared. We need to make some noise."

They aim for the towers and start to pelt the bells with shots. These add up and the bells begin to resonate through the town square. Suddenly the congregation moves out of the building to a sight they have never imagined: teams of armed African teenagers, several pointing arrows at them.

The Portuguese sergeant, a large man with a scarred face, comes to the front of the crowd.

"What is this?"

With his commanding voice booming across the city square Zumbi responds:

"These are the sons and daughters of freedom who came to rescue their brothers and sisters."

"What type of madness is this?" says the sergeant, wide-eyed.

The priest comes out and tries to pledge with Zumbi:

"My son, put down your arrows."

"Father, if you actually followed Christ's words, you would come to join our side. If you continue to bless these sinners, you will end up like Saint Sebastian."

A few in the audience from inside the church laugh at this threat. Zumbi continues unperturbed.

"Enough blood has been spilled today. Your foremen are dead or captured. I will let you all go back to Recife with your wagons. You can take a wagon and a horse per family."

The sergeant quickly counts the force in front of him. He knows his battalion is not enough.

"Where are my men?"

"Your men are waiting for your order. Tell them to leave their weapons behind and come out. Nobody else needs to get hurt."

The sergeant is a practical man. Having engaged with the Dutch forces and some Tupi tribes, he knows when to settle and surrender. He can feel Zumbi has control of the situation—and the town.

"We leave the weapons, but the farmers get to take their cattle and furniture with them."

Andala, Yakini, and Antonio Soares gather with Zumbi to decide.

"We should not allow them to take anything," says Antonio Soares.

"Can you imagine if we arrive back with so many freed Africans and some cattle?" says Andala.

Yakini is quiet.

"No," says Zumbi.

They look at him waiting for some reason not to make this victory even bigger.

"We should not push our luck or corner our enemies into desperation. Let them take their stuff, we will keep the village. We are not thieves, we are conquerors."

"He is right. We need to give them a chance to surrender with some dignity," says Yakini.

In the meantime, the sergeant is inside the church convincing the farmers to let go, take the cattle, and leave. Several want to stay and fight. They have pistols in their belts, but some have wives and daughters who do not want them to take the risk. In the end, the priest helps them come to terms with surrender the Christian way: through guilt. When they come out, Zumbi is ready with his plan for their departure to Recife.

"We will send men who worked in each farm to load your carriages and wagons. They will drive these loaded wagons here and you will have to drive them from here. These men and women are now free. You owe them payment for their work so we will take your houses and land."

At this sound of impeccable logic, the Portuguese give up arguing and the newly freed Africans celebrate. They are ready now to take possession of their new houses and farms. After a few uncomfortable hours the newly freed Africans return with full wagons and broad smiles. They also bring cattle and a few horses. Amid the furniture and clothes are the tied foremen.

The Portuguese families get in their wagons and move out. Many are brutal and do not speak to their freed men and women. A few say short goodbyes. There is one whose couple extend hands and shake in respectful silence. There is a deep resignation among the Portuguese: these are families that crossed an ocean looking for fortune and now have to face shame and defeat. Deep inside their surrender is also recognition that there is no defense imaginable for the horror of slavery and merciless exploitation of a people.

***

Yakini

During this brief reconciliation, one of the Portuguese troops points his musket at Zumbi. Everything passes very quickly. The man takes aim and pulls the trigger; the only one to see it is Yakini who, with no hesitation, jumps in front of the shot. She is hit, her body absorbing the charge, and falls to the ground.

With two jumps Pintada reaches the shooter, gets to his neck, and kills him. All the other Portuguese troops put their hands up in surrender while the young African warriors hold their bows and swords. Zumbi runs to Yakini's fallen body. She is bleeding fast and dying faster. They both know that. Zumbi's long planned and carefully executed success seems to crumble and fall in a fraction of a minute. He holds her in her final moments, moments that bring him the image of his mother bleeding to death when he was born—and from now on those images will be linked in his mind.

"No!" cries Zumbi.

"It does not hurt, my prince," says Yakini.

"No, please do not die."

"Fear not, my prince. The plan was good. The Portuguese man was treacherous."

"You were the bravest among us."

"I still am." She smiles.

"You are the bravest among us."

"And you are my prince. Always." Yakini says no more.

"I still am, I still am …" Zumbi sobs.

And responding to his words, she is just silence. Yakini, who with Zumbi, Antonio, Soares and Andala, made up the "four horsemen of the trivium" according to some, is no more. Her death marks the end of childhood for all of them. All those childhood adventures the four of them had, which became legend among African youth in the Americas, now belong to the ages.

Zumbi remembers their first day at the trivium classes when she was so eager to learn, and how she bested them all in the skills of capoeira. The beautiful, smart, hard-working Yakini is the one casualty in the conquering of Garanhuns. Zumbi learns bitter lessons at this moment. That one's love cannot protect those one loves, no matter how much one loves them. That in a moment a great victory can turn into a tragic defeat. That the best plans can bring grief even when they succeed.

Andala and Antonio Soares join them and the four of them are together for one last time.

"Take her to the church, and leave a team guarding it."

After the Portuguese settlers move out of the village, the teens start to set the town square and the houses surrounding it on fire. They are wildly celebrating their improbable wild victory mixed with anger for the killing of Yakini.

"Stop them," says Zumbi.

"But why?" asks Antonio Soares. "They are burning a Portuguese settlement."

"No. They are burning our new village. This will be named Tapera."

"Tapera?"

"That is Tupi for 'vanquished city.' Both Portuguese and Tupi will get the message. It is ours now and we need to take good care of it."

The extent of Zumbi's ambition starts to become clear in his friend's mind.

"You wanted this all along … we did not come here to free these enslaved people; we came to conquer a stronghold."

"Do you see how this village is located? Remember the Gospel: a city that is set on a hill cannot be hidden. If we stay vigilant, a small group will be able to defend this."

"The Portuguese could not defend it from us."

"That is because they underestimated our force. They thought of themselves as invincible. We will not make the same mistake about them."

Zumbi opens a faint smile and moves to stop their teams from destroying his new village, Pintada following him closely. They need to prepare the defense and occupation of Garanhuns, now Tapera, and plan their return to Palmares. Before they do, they must organize Yakini's burial following their tradition of marking the battlefield with the tombs of those who fell there.

"We will bury her under the first row of this church," Zumbi orders, and nobody questions him.

***

The return is a triumph with the class adding not one person, not one family, but thirty families to Palmares, plus the twenty families that stayed behind to take care of the farms and reorganize Tapera as the new addition to Palmares.

Instead of joining the celebration, Zumbi goes straight to Yakini's family hut and presents her parents with her sword. Zumbi is sober as he embraces them, and they exchange few words.

* * *

A few months later as they are reading Plutarch's stories on Alexander, one of the students jests to the class: "The teenager Alexander conquered the horse Bucephalus, the teenager Zumbi conquered Garanhuns."

Italian Interlude: Bologna, 1670

Galileo turned the telescope from the enemy at the distance to the stars in the sky. He has been dead now for almost thirty years. Now it is time to turn the microscope to the parts of the human body and beyond, including to the parts of animals and even plants.

This fellow Italian sees the great chain of being forming, though it will still take two centuries for Darwin and Wallace to put all together. By studying humans alongside animals and plants he founds comparative anatomy, though the field of study remains unnamed. He is also founding, at the same time, embryology, physiology, and histology.

In putting the skin under the microscope to find the origin of the dark tones, he discovers the location of the pigment that colors the dermis of Africans. Otherwise, the anatomy is absolutely the same. Skin color is only skin color. The difference is made up by the eyes of those whose mind want to see more. The color of every other organ is the same. Under the microscope he finds no other difference.

A few years past he received a letter from London by a Mr. Oldenburg of the Royal Society. He is now a member of the society and is finishing his masterpiece, "The Anatomy of Plants." In it, he draws what he sees under the microscope, naming structures along the way. Inside animals, people, and plants, he sees vistas never suspected by the naked eye. A new continent is thus discovered.

He spends most of his life in his birthplace of Bologna, until the pope asks him to move to Rome and serve as his personal physician. He dies three years later. At his request, an autopsy is performed in his body.

His tomb at the church of the Santi Gregorio e Siro, in Bologna, reads

> "SUMMUM INGENIUM / INTEGERRIMAM VITAM / FORTEM STRENUAMQUE MENTEM / AUDACEM SALUTARIS ARTIS AMOREM":

great genius, honest life, strong and tough mind, daring love for the medical art.

His name is Marcello Malpighi.

CHAPTER 10

NIGHTS AT THE CIRCUS

1671
A Test of Endurance

At the end of training, the weapons and combat class has one individual final test: survive alone for a whole month in the wild with no outside help. This is called the self-reliance test, a test of endurance and survival, a test for facing all fears combined: loneliness, cold nights, rainy days, hunger, and above all the fear of failing and falling short of expectations—their own and those of their parents and community. This is the test that will release boys in the jungle and welcome back men ready for battle, let girls go into the wild and welcome back women, also ready for battle. In the Free Republic of Palmares, women take part in battle.

"I do not have the luxury of leaving half my people hiding at home," said an exasperated Ganga Zumba one day.

His advisors were skeptical, but this command was not put up for a vote or even discussion.

"Those women who want to fight should be given a weapon. Now. Those men who are cowards can stay back in the village."

Many Black women came forward and joined the legions. No Black man returned to the village.

Now, another weapons and combat training class meets at the west field after the quadrivium lectures every day and works till nightfall. Even those youth who did not qualify for the higher education of the trivium or the quadrivium have to learn to fight.

This night, for their final test, they bring all their equipment: one group has swords, knives, spears; a second carries bows and arrows; a third slings; and a fourth small group carries muskets. A handful of students has a combined assortment of all the weapons. These are the special commanders, for in order to command all troops, they learn all weapons. Members of the royal families are expected to be in the commander group.

"A good leader works harder than those who follow" is one of Ganga-Zumba's favorite sayings.

Zumbi appears with his sword hanging down his left leg; a sling on the right; his knife attached to his right arm, as if a new muscle between his biceps and triceps; his bow crossing his torso; his quiver on his back crossing with his spear. His dark hair is long now and hangs down around his face like a lion's mane. He exudes physical power and would be menacing if not for his easy broad smile. Andala and Antonio Soares are also carrying all weapons, except they also each have a musket with them.

"Where is your musket, Prince Zumbi?" asks the Moor.

"Do you think with all these weapons I still need a musket?" He spreads his arms wide, his hands pointing to his back, exposing the knife in his arm, bow and spear crossing behind his shoulder, sword hanging on one side, and sling on the other. Now his broad smile turns into laughter and almost closes his eyes. Humor is contagious among those that are anxious. The Moor does not respond and turns to speak to the whole group.

"Each of you will go out alone tonight. It is the first night of a full moon. You can only return in the next full moon. There will be many nights ahead. You should be alone. I know each of you. You are prepared. The forest will feed you, if you do your part. The forest will take care of you, if you do your part. Hunt, gather, move, be safe, be smart.

"You are Black women and men. Your ancestors survived crossing the ocean and survived slavery; they founded this kingdom in defiance of the mighty Portuguese. You are their fruit, their children and grandchildren born here, free. When you return you will be the men and women of Palmares."

"Free Palmares! Free Palmares!" the group responds, many voices merging into one cry.

The group disperses, students moving toward the tropical wilderness. Antonio Soares, Andala, and Zumbi are the last to go—the three in the commander group, heavy with weapons.

"Good luck, Princes."

"Good luck, Antonio."

They give each other the Palmares salute, clapping their hands, and depart into the forest and into the night. Students spread all over the woods and mountains around the five villages. Each of them knows where the streams and waterfalls are, and most importantly, they know where the best caves and hideouts are located. The rule is that the first to a spot can occupy it for the month. There is a race to the best spots. Those who completed the quadrivium class can also use the stars as guides at night.

Zumbi goes a different direction and has a plan of his own: he wants to see the ocean. Since he was a little boy, he heard stories of the infinite expanse of green and blue waters that is the ocean in these coasts. When he was young, he would dream of being able to swim so much he would reach Angola on the other side of the world.

The plains between the mountains, where Palmares is located, and the seashore, where the Portuguese are, form the borderlands for Palmares. The coast, crawling with Portuguese. is always a forbidden land. One never knows when a caravel may show up, or when a group of soldiers—or worse yet *capitaes-do-mato*—will show up. But Zumbi knows the coast is long and the Portuguese, now that they have Recife, prefer its lazy streets to the rough sandy trails. He also knows stories about the ferocious Goytacazes, a Native Brazilian tribe so savage that neither the Portuguese nor the Tupi could defeat them. The Goytacazes live somewhere on the coast.

Zumbi walks, Pintada at his side, always heading east. After a day moving, they sleep embraced by a hillside. The full moon is still floating the second night, illuminating everything. The solitude makes the night long and darker despite the full moon, and they sleep next to each other. Another day, another long walk. Stretches of land upon land, between the hills that become smaller as they approach the coast. Each night they make dinner with fruit and pieces of a wild turkey Pintada caught as they walked through a clearing.

One morning as the rosy fingers of dawn break the day, Zumbi awakes and realizes he can see the ocean in the distance. They had found their sleeping place after nightfall, so they had not realized the day before that they were so close to the beach. From this distance he sees for the first time the open vistas of the Atlantic Ocean. He wants to run toward it, so immense and infinite is the vision, as a blue canvas spread on the horizon.

Their pace is quickened and they cover ground as fast as they can, reaching the seaside by the end of the day. As they approach, they make sure it is an isolated beach, no Portuguese or Tupi footprints anywhere. This is virgin sand.

The full moon rises in the horizon as the sun sets on their backs. A young Black man, strong and tall, and a young jaguar, majestic and quiet, step for the first time into the white sands of this South American Atlantic coastal stretch.

It takes time for their feet, and paws, to get used to the shifting sands. Then, it is a final race toward the shore. The sounds of the ocean fill their ears. The salty smell inaugurates a new sensation. Salty air, breathing in and breathing out. They run to the surf. Zumbi looks at the waves breaking, their sound whooshing to their ears, whispering, "Come on, come in."

One thought invades his mind: *These are the same waters that touch Africa, the same water! If only I could swim this distance. Home is on the other shoulder of this blue titan.*

He finds some coconut trees and hides his equipment, except for his knife, still attached to his arm. He goes for a swim, the salty taste now in his mouth. Pintada looks at him, unsure whether she wants to join in this mad dash into these unruled waters. She goes, eventually—and only tentatively.

Zumbi swims, and the water gets deeper. He goes under, he comes back up. The waves break on his face and he laughs. He yells to the heavens, "Thank you!" He submerges and tries to open his eyes in the deep. The salty water hurts and burns, and he comes up. He laughs. The water seems to have no end; the waves keep moving. Pintada is swimming next to him, her head just above water. Night falls. He still wants to swim after dinner. This time Pintada firmly stays behind, guarding their small campsite.

He loves the water and at night it feels like a warm embrace as the cold wind brushes the beachside. As he goes in and out of the deep, he thinks he sees a human form ahead of him. A girl's head appears and disappears close to him, as if by magic. He goes down, tries to see it. One time he goes under and sees a large fishtail. Going back up he sees the girl's head, her long hair floating on the surface.

"Come here!" he says.

The vision disappears for good now. A dream, a mirage, a hallucination—nothing is clear. How can one know all that is possible in an endless water world? He remembers the legends of sirens and mermaids in Homer's *Odyssey*. He is too exhausted now and swims back. The border between night and day, water and land, sleep and awareness seems to be shifting now.

Zumbi and Pintada go to sleep by the coconut trees. He has heard about these strange green balls that have fresh water inside them. He cuts the first one with one quick sword hit; the coconut explodes and the water is lost. Eventually he uses his knife and carves a hole in one. He gets for the first time the sweet tasting coconut water. They drink, then finish the wild turkey. Tomorrow he plans to try spearfishing. Tonight, he knows his dreams will not be any stranger than this gigantic salty lake dancing in front of them.

***

Visitors on the Beach

Morning comes, the sun's rays pushing the night away. Zumbi opens his eyes and sees a giant face, wide-open eyes over a long beard, staring at him. Is he still sleeping? In the distance he hears Pintada roaring furiously. Is this a dream? He closes his eyes hoping it will go away. He opens them again and the giant is still there, looking straight at him. They startle each other.

"The boy is alive!" yells the huge man.

Zumbi jumps and his eyes check for his weapons. He can see they are still next to the coconut trees and his knife is still attached to his arm.

"Who are you?"

The man in front of him is over seven feet tall. An extreme height, no matter what time or place.

"I am William Bradley! The Yorkshire Giant!" He laughs with a belly-deep satisfaction.

"Have I gone insane?" says Zumbi.

In Palmares Zumbi is among the tallest men, close to six feet. He never imagined a man could be over seven feet tall. As he adjusts to this man in front of him, who moves quite slowly, a much quicker and shorter person comes from behind the giant.

"Hi! Hello! I am Franco Albion! Don't you hurt my giant!"

"I am Zumbi dos Palmares! What type of people are you? Who are you?"

"Oh! You are one of those escaped slaves in this area? They told me there would be some. But they said they are weak and scared. They also said you are all starving to death. You do not look starved."

"I am not a slave nor enslaved. I was born free."

"Nobody is born free in this world, my friend. Listen, do you know about the circus?"

"The what?"

"The circus! We entertain people: for a few coins we will give you a spectacle! I am the ringmaster of the Albion Circus, the greatest show on earth! We are on our way to Recife!"

Zumbi eyes him with a serious and suspicious look.

"Where is my jaguar?"

"Oh, that is yours? I thought we could bring it with us?"

Zumbi takes out his knife. Albion looks at it.

"Not worth this kind of fight. Let the cat go!" he yells.

Someone in the background releases Pintada who runs to Zumbi's side.

"So, what you doing here?"

Zumbi is still suspicious. This strange man and his strange giant are something he has never seen before. Yet their open attitude and broad smile helps him trust them.

"I just came to check out the coast. I wanted to see the ocean."

"Well, we are going to stop here for a few days, rehearse our numbers, get ready for Recife. The big city on these shores!"

He gestures as fast as he talks, and he appears never to stop doing either.

The day passes with Zumbi watching the coast and the ocean while Albion's crew sets up their encampment. Zumbi sees several wagons and a few people walking back and forth. Most of the wagons are covered and look like little houses on wheels. Two others are huge wooden boxes: one containing a weary-looking lion and another with three sides made of wood and one large front glass panel. The glass container is full of water. Pintada spends the day checking the lion's wagon from the distance while Zumbi tries to decide between going back to the forest or enjoying more of the ocean, even with the constant noise and presence of this strange group.

"What are these?" Zumbi asks Albion.

"There are my two main attractions. The lion has been with me for years. I bought him in Africa."

Zumbi thinks about the captives that arrive at Palmares who lived long enough in Africa to remember its colors and flavors. Zumbi used to pester them with questions about all details of life and things in Africa. Now he is looking at an African lion.

"This beast was once a mighty hunter in the African steppes," Zumbi wonders out loud.

"He was indeed. I believe he is now twenty years of age, and they say they live to be about fifteen in the wild. I promised myself I would keep him for five years then let him go."

"Are you going to set him free?"

"I tried once, believe me. The weird thing was, when we opened the cage to let him go, he remained there. We tried and tried, but it appears he feels safe in there. He is now so used to life behind bars that he did not care for the open fields in front of him."

"Some people are like that: they prefer the safety of captivity to the freedom of taking care of themselves."

"Indeed. So I kept him in my circus. We feed him daily, he comes out for our shows, then he goes right back up to his cage."

The old lion seems bored in the cage. From time to time it paces back and forth, but most of the time it appears to doze on and off. Looking at him and Pintada, one could see the proud, healthy, muscular body of the wild jaguar and the saggy body of the captive lion.

"How about the other wagon? The one with water?"

"I have a very special attraction for this one. A very special young woman who can hold her breath longer than any man. She is my mermaid."

At lunch, Albion and his crew eat on a large canvas spread on the sand. It looks like a huge caravel sail flat on the ground. They gesture for Zumbi to join them. He walks slowly, Pintada by his side, checking for possible traps.

"So, kid, you are part of this quilombo, yes?"

"I am. And I am thinking about whether I should let you go to Recife now that you know where I am." Zumbi's weapons shine in the bright tropical sun.

"Listen, I do not care about where you are or your folks are! That is not my fight and I am not up for starting even my own fights, let alone those of others! Besides, my wife is Black! From Africa! Do you see any slaves here? There are none! We are artists and performers; we don't care to have people doing things for us. We take care of ourselves."

Zumbi looks at him, ponders, and eats.

"So, you met William, the Yorkshire Giant, and me," Albion says. "Now you see Pedro Jose, our juggler, and Julia, our belly dancer."

Pedro and Julia sit next to each other. They smile and wave to him.

"Catarina, my wife, is the real boss here. She is in the covered wagon, checking the books, preparing the food, and watching over our daughter."

"May I talk to her?" Zumbi asks, receiving as a response a suspicious, inquisitive look from Albion.

"You said she is Black," Zumbi explains.

Albion finishes sucking on a chicken bone, licks his fingers, and look back at him.

"Sure. But we have to go to the wagon. She does not come out in this burning sun."

They finish eating and walk to the covered wagon. As they approach, Albion yells, "Catarina! I have got a guest with me!"

Zumbi stops and waits.

"Tell him to come in" a female voice echoes from the covered wagon.

As Zumbi enters the wagon the smell of paper seems overwhelming. Notes, books, journals: it feels like a collection of old parchments and papers. Lying in a colorful bed of sheets and curtains is the whitest person he has ever seen.

"Are you Catarina?"

"Yes. And my husband told me your name is Zumbi."

"It is, and he told me you are Black."

"I am."

The puzzled look on his face only continues to grow. The more he looks at her, the more confused he is. She does have thick, sensuous lips and a broad nose, but her skin is white like the moon. Not only white like Portuguese or Dutch—she is almost transparent. Zumbi can see the markings of veins in her arms.

"The Portuguese call us albinos," Catarina says.

"Albinos?"

"Yes, some say we are cursed, some say we are blessed. I say we are people."

"Where from?"

"I was born in Angola, but my family was afraid of my white skin and pink eyes. There are others like this in my family, born a generation ago. Some were killed so their organs could be used in magic potions. Some ran away and live in the forest. My father took me to Luanda and sold me to a Portuguese trader."

"And how did you end up with this crew?"

"One day the circus came to my town and Albion took an interest in me. He likes freaks, I guess. He talks too much but he is a good man. He bought me and married me. Not like others, by forcing me to bed. He freed me and said, 'You can go.' I wanted to stay."

"So, there are Portuguese people like that? Who free those enslaved instead of keeping them in chains?"

"Yes, Zumbi. There are such Portuguese, more than you think. This is a beautiful yet cruel land and it brings out the worst in people. But there are plenty of Portuguese who feel the injustices of the world. Not much to do, though. We all have to live in the time we are allotted."

Black people who are white, Portuguese people who do not believe in slavery. The education of encountering others is happening to the African prince, and as usual the best education happens when you do not know you are being educated.

Twilight colors the sky pink in the west, the sun setting behind the green mountains in the distance, while the night comes from the east, the full moon still hanging in the sky. The roar of the South Atlantic becomes background music to everything they do.

At dusk the crew sets up a table. Zumbi comes with Pintada, bringing fish and a few crabs. Night starts to embrace them all and a bonfire is set.

"You two can fish!" Albion exclaims as he looks at the arrows and spear. "How about we give these fish to the cats and let the crabs boil?"

Zumbi nods.

William, Pedro Jose, Julia, and Albion are together around the table getting everything ready. Catarina comes out, fully covered with scarves in what looks like a colorful toga. She sits by Zumbi. The food is good. Albion picks up a very small Portuguese guitar, which in Brazil is known as *cavaquinho* and which one day will travel to Hawaii and be named *ukulele*. The tune they play is not a happy one. It oozes painful resignation to one's lot. William has a deep singing voice that matches his incredible size, and Pedro Jose follows him a few octaves higher. Julia dances, and her moves only confirm the melancholy of the melody and the words speaking of love, loss, longing, and death. One day these songs will give birth to a style known as *fado* meaning fate, the inescapable power of one's destiny. It expresses the deep sadness of the Portuguese soul.

> *Longing for you and for your presence*
> *That now only lives in my memories*
> *Of the days we had together*
> *Of the nights we had each other*
> *Longing for you and for your love*
> *That now is only a remembrance*
> *Of the days we had together*
> *Of the nights we had each other*
> *You are gone and I am still here*
> *Failing to make sense of the world*
> *Days are dark and nights are long*
> *Longing for you and for your love*

As they sit at the dinner table, a bottle of Portuguese wine goes around. This Portuguese feast brings so much to the eyes, the skin, the mouth, the ears. This is a cauldron of sadness, hope, love, fear—enough to overflow one's heart and soul. That is Portugal.

Catarina opens a big smile.

"I finally get a fellow Black person among these people!" She laughs and they laugh too. She seems truly happy to have him with them. Zumbi is serious, trying to decide if he should rescue her from this company of strange people.

"Albion told me you have a daughter?"

"Yes."

Zumbi waits for more. The question is hard to ask so he remains silent.

"Is she Black or White, is that the question that is stuck on your tongue? That is what folks most want to know." She has had this conversation many times before.

Zumbi nods.

"When I had a child with a white man, I thought she would be white, like I am white, at least in my skin. Then when she came to the world, they brought me the most beautiful brown little girl. We raise her like a criollo woman but I know she is half Black. One can tell these things; a mother can for sure. The blood has memory and despite my pale skin, the blood's memory is Black."

"Where is she? I would like to meet her."

Albion who is taking part in all conversations around the table at the same time, interjects, still speaking fast.

"She is swimming! She loves to swim at night! In the ocean! Can you believe that? You, me, most of us spend our days on dry land, getting into the water here and there. She is the opposite! She spends her days in water, coming to dry land here and there! She is my mermaid!"

As they finish the meal the group divides: William and Albion in one direction, Julia and Pedro Jose to their wagon. Catarina and Zumbi stay at the table. Zumbi senses someone approaching behind him.

"Here she is! Our mermaid!" Albion yells as if he is introducing the show. "You know she challenges any man or woman in the water tank—our mermaid tank. She holds her breath longer than any person on the planet!"

***

Yara

Zumbi turns around and sees a beautiful woman walking toward them. She has big bright-green eyes and her pitch-black long wet hair drips water on her soaked clothes. Her skin is dark brown, lighter than her hair, and she cuts a stunning figure. She is short with a narrow waist but broad hips and strong muscular legs. Her firm breasts press on her wet shirt.

Zumbi keeps quiet, not knowing what to say. His eyes grow large in the presence of such beauty. He notices his heart beating fast. Taking a seat by her mother, she eats with the appetite of one who passes the time exercising. At the end she looks at Zumbi and asks with a smile, "Want to go swimming?" Her tone is innocent, as if swimming were the equivalent of a stroll on the beach.

Zumbi looks at her parents. They nod their trusting approval: the circus itinerant life, and their own mixed marriage, has freed them of so many prejudices and mores that people carry in their hearts and heads.

The two young bodies head for the water. The moon gives enough light to clearly see as they approach the surf and each other.

"I did not catch your name."

"My name is Yara. Yara Albion." Then she jumps in the water, disappearing into the waves.

Zumbi jumps in and swims toward her. Few words are needed, and none are spoken.

They swim and dive, finding each other under water and coming back up together. They embrace, they swim again. Waves come and go, throwing them toward one another. The crew is now back in conversation at the dinner table; only Pintada and Catarina are observing them from the shore in the distance.

Whales

Together they swim until the shore is just a faint note on the horizon behind them. They stop, look at each other, and laugh. Night does not wait to fall, and in a few instants the sun is just a forgotten memory on the horizon. At this moment, Zumbi realizes he cannot touch the ground even when he dives as deep as his lungs allow. He resurfaces and sees Yara, who is not bothered. He is. He has been to rivers where one cannot reach the bottom, but at least one can always see the banks on each side: reminders of dry land.

"Let us swim back," he says.

"I want you to see something," Yara responds.

"What?"

As he finishes his question, he feels a push from below, a force driving him upward, as if a gigantic bull were ramming him; he is pushed above the waterline into the night air. The animal lifting him is an enormous mass of muscle, larger than any other live being he has ever seen.

Zumbi recovers his balance and stands up for an instant over the sea waters. The animal dives back in, and he falls back into the water. Yara watches the spectacle, laughing like a child.

"I knew they would do that!" she says.

"What is that? What kind of monster is this?"

"These are not monsters, silly. These are whales. There are many of them around us right now."

So that is what you wanted me to see?"

"Of course."

"Are they dangerous?"

"No, they are kind, and funny, and like to play," she says, speaking fast like her father. "Every time I swim in these waters during these months, I see several of them, usually in pairs. They have never hurt me."

Now Zumbi wants the whale to return. The whale does, but not alone. Now they are a pair. Yara rides on one and Zumbi on the other. The whales play with them as they swim, leaping with their riders into the air. As the young couple swims back to shore, the two whales execute several jumps behind them as if saying, "Come back tomorrow to play again." And they promise themselves they will.

Happily tired, they swim to find a landing in a patch of sand distant enough from the vigilant eye of Yara's mother. The magnetic power of two young bodies who grew up alone—Zumbi, a prince to whom all in the quilombo keep a respectful distance, and Yara, whose traveling family does not stop in any place for long—is indomitable.

They embrace under the full moon, covered in salty water, as if they need each other to breathe out of water. Nature has its ways to teach love, and young bodies learn fast. The full moon bathes them and their love is pure and animal. Zumbi smells Yara's neck and kisses her face, his hands running through her hair. Her hands pull his muscular body toward hers, not afraid that its touch feels so good. Finally, she grabs his face and kisses him, and they surrender to each other in abandon.

***

This becomes their routine all week: as the moon comes up, dinner is served, and a nocturnal swim is inevitable. They cannot help finding so much comfort from each other's bodies, time and again.

Like the *fados* they sing, destiny comes at the end of the full moon, when the troupe has to continue their march to Recife and Zumbi has to return to Palmares. They know they likely will never see each other again. And they know there is nothing can they do in this implacable world. They have had their time and it will remain imprinted in their memories. Zumbi has his duty to his people. Yara has her family to take care of. Theirs is not an age for tearful goodbyes but of quiet resignation—and they are, like all of us, products of their age.

But Yara will see Zumbi's face again nine months later, when she gives birth to a dark-skinned baby boy. They name him Joao Pedro. Three quarters African, one quarter Portuguese: a rough sketch of Brazil, drafted one hundred and fifty years before the country itself comes to existence.

Albion and Catarina love their first and only grandchild. They know and worry about his fate in this land where Portuguese feed on the blood of Africans. Yet they love Recife, the lovely and painfully beautiful Brazilian northeast coast. Eventually they move northwest to a region that one day will be known as Ceará. In this new province the beaches are sandy and the waters green, more beautiful and less cruel than Pernambuco, where they leave one great friend: a free-woman named Anna M.

German Interlude: Mainz , 1671

They knew he was a prodigy way back in 1661 when he started university studies in Leipzig at the age of fifteen. There, he wrote about theology and mathematics, eventually receiving a doctoral degree in law at the age of twenty. Now twenty-five, he writes two treaties: one dedicated to Académie des Sciences de Paris and a second to the Royal Society in London. He also designs a calculating machine called the "Step Reckoner," the first to perform all four arithmetic operations.

Next year he will be given the opportunity of a lifetime: a diplomatic mission to Paris. In Paris he will meet the intellectual leaders of the age: Antoine Arnauld, Nicholas Malebranche, and Dutch mathematician and physicist Christiaan Huygens. After four years in France, he will make his way back to Germany, passing through Amsterdam and visiting Spinoza.

Throughout his life he will write on mathematics, logic, theology, and natural philosophy, and he will independently develop calculus simultaneous with Isaac Newton. He is an optimist and dreams of reconciling religions, in particular the chasm between Protestants and Catholics. In this he will fail.

Of him the French intellectual giant Diderot will say: *When one compares the talents one has with those of him, one is tempted to throw away one's books and go die quietly in the dark of some forgotten corner.*

Of him his German compatriot mathematician Gottlob Frege will say: *In his writings, he threw out such a profusion of seeds of ideas that in this respect he is virtually in a class of his own.*

His name is Gottfried Wilhelm Leibniz.

Chapter 11

Love and Loss

1672

Zumbi returns to Palmares changed and confused by the encounter with Yara. He had known love with Acirema for
years, but these nights had shown him something different:
maybe some unsuspected layers of love. A love that felt free
and carnal, different from anything he has ever experienced
or dreamed existed. The meeting with Yara opened a door to
a dimension that once entered, allows for no return.

"I feel I am no longer a hollow man, no longer a stuffed
man. There is something else inside," Zumbi says to Antonio
Soares.

"Man, you came back strange from this challenge. You
were strange before, but now …!"

"I know. I am strange even to myself. I am no longer
empty, I am full. Funny thing is, I did not know I was empty
before. I just know now I am full, in ways I cannot deny."

"Full of what?"

"Energy? Movement? Vigor? Life!"

All that he says to his friend Antonio; the challenge is
what to say to Acirema. However, when Zumbi meets her,

there is nothing to be said and no words needed. Whatever had possessed him immediately jumps into her, and she is as ready as he. Their love, which had rested in their eyes and hands for years, now moves to their whole bodies. And now, when they escape to find each other for the first night, after swimming in a stream under the night sky, they do not just watch each other's breath in sleep. They love.

But what is love? Love is not static; it is always in movement inside and outside the bodies of the loving and the loved. Love is alive as much in the guts as in the soul, like a bridge linking the animal and the divine. And after lying down with an enchanted mermaid, in sands no longer pristine, Zumbi returns to Palmares transformed by this new love, whose presence inside him tormented him not only at night or in dreams but during the day in his waking hours.

Now when his eyes meet Acirema's, he sees no longer the little companion of childhood play, but a young woman whose legs are fit not only for games and races. Now there is in her a promise of acceptance, refuge, pleasure, joy, and happiness. The carnality that had spared them so long came with the irresistible power of a dammed river whose wall had just exploded.

***

That first night becomes another, then another. Although their secret routine is altered, Zumbi continues to spend his days in trivium classes followed by quadrivium then weapons and combat. When night comes, instead of joining the other boys at their hut, Zumbi and Acirema elope to each other. At each opportunity, they find each other in the night and walk, almost running, toward their secret place by the stream, Pintada serving as their silent night watch.

These nights are happy nights, nights of love and sleep and rest and dreaming of a life together in which all nights will be a repetition of these nights, a never-ending string of loving nights. These are their dreams, and as young people before them and since, they believe that dreaming together will make them come true. Somehow.

In the waking hours, that never-ending string of nights stops when Acirema misses her period. At first, they do not know what to say to each other. Life finds its ways, and now there is a new life growing inside her. Zumbi is so happy, tears fall from his eyes as he tentatively touches her belly, now a sacred place. He smiles, she beams, they embrace in the deep affection, passion, and innocence of young love.

"I need to tell my uncle," he says.

Her smile turns into a frown.

"Wait a few days, let us be sure."

She gets sick in the mornings now. There is little room for doubt; even others around her start to suspect her pregnancy.

"I will talk to my uncle tomorrow."

She nods.

They spend that night together. She stays all night in his arms and tells him Tupi legends about the night sky that she learned from her father. He, in turn, tells her African legends about how Black people came to be. They promise to always think of each other when the full moon is illuminating the night. Acirema sleeps, and he carefully synchronizes his breathing with hers to make sure he does not wake her. And then he spends most of the night watching her sleep.

"I promise."

Next day Zumbi asks for an audience with Ganga Zumba, king and uncle. He requests time alone with his uncle, a privilege few people have with the sovereign. They meet at the ruler's private quarters.

"Uncle …"

Zumbi is rarely tentative and Ganga Zumba notices he is having a difficult time finding the words.

"I am here for you, prince. What is going on?"

"It is a girl."

"A girl?"

"Yes. We have been seeing each other."

"In these nocturnal escapades my sentinels tell me about? They see you escaping many a night to the forest."

There is pride in the king's tone.

"She is pregnant." Zumbi pauses. "We believe she is."

The king's tone changes and he takes a deep breath. Pride is now replaced by calculations—political calculations.

"Who is she?"

"Acirema."

"Tuibae's daughter?"

"Yes."

The mood in the room shifts. The king is now furious, his royal temper out in the open, his eyes blazing at Zumbi.

"She is a half-breed, a mixed race, a mongrel! Half Tupi, half African."

Zumbi's surprise, fear, and disappointment are displayed in his wide eyes and open mouth.

"But—"

"No *but*! No respect! You are a prince of Palmares! You are an African prince. You must act like one."

"Uncle—"

"Before your uncle, I am a king, your king. Before my nephew, you are a prince. Princes do not have the luxury of love! You cannot be spreading bastards around our communities! Your seed and your blood are to be part of our family's arrangements. You will marry the daughter of a chief, not the product of an African woman who shares her hammock with a blind Tupi man."

Zumbi wants to cry but now his pride holds down his tears. Ganga Zumba continues.

"We shall send them out. Maybe to Amaro ... no, to Osenga. This meeting is over. You may leave now. I will make the proper arrangements. The Moor will see that the whole family is moved quietly and quickly."

Zumbi leaves the palace in a state of confusion. People talk to him but he cannot make sense of what they say. He needs to find Acirema. He now plans to escape with her to another citadel, maybe to the forest, and start a new community where people can love and live truly free from these family entanglements. Maybe they can move back to the Tupi lands, find Tuibae's tribe. He runs to Acirema's family hut, Pintada fast at his side.

He finds Tuibae's hut empty, except for a brief note written in Acirema's neat handwriting, a note whose words will be carved in his heart to the end of his days:

If it is to ruin both our lives versus to ruin just mine, let me ruin mine alone. I will never be alone again now that I have a piece of you with me. Love. Always. Remember the moon promise.

He screams in despair, around him only solitude and silence. The empty hut, the village going about its business as if nothing has happened, when his life has just changed forever. Nothing makes sense. Worse yet, all his pain will be suffered in secret and isolation, for he cannot utter any of this sad tale to anyone. It is a pain that cannot be shared or expressed except for his long-hidden tears.

Zumbi runs to the end of Macaco, to the big gate and guard house.

"Have you seen Tuibae and his family? Did they pass by here?"

"Yes, my prince. They walked by with a few possessions on a mule. We thought they were moving to another citadel."

"Gone, gone. They are gone." The words go round and round in Zumbi's head. The guards look at each other, not knowing what to say or do.

Zumbi and Pintada run into the forest but there are so many pathways and tracks it is impossible to catch them. "Gone, gone. They are gone," continues to resonate in his mind. They end up spending the night alone in one of the secret hideouts where Zumbi and Acirema had spent nights of love. This is just the first of many nights he will find refuge in isolation and darkness. That pain that cannot be shared tears him up inside.

That day Acirema and her family start on the path back to the Tupi lands where her father is a distant memory. To the Tupi, Tuibae returns now with an African wife and beautiful daughter whose pregnancy starts to show. The Tupi welcome him back, the old blind man with wild stories and now a mixed family. When Tuibae had first moved to Palmares, he taught the Africans about the Tupi language and customs. Now back from Palmares, he teaches the Tupi about how the Africans talk, how they think, and how they live together.

The Tupi lands are vast and occupy the central plains and hinterlands of Brazil. Tuibae decides to settle with Zuleika and Acirema in a settlement near the broad river that cuts the hinterland in half and one day will be named after Saint Francis by the Portuguese. That river is like a narrow angry ocean in the middle of the desert.

There they will live, and there Kauan is born six month later. The boy is three-quarters African and one quarter Tupi, for those who live by measuring blood. For the Tupi he will be a dark-skinned Tupi warrior, the bravest of his tribe. He has the green eyes of Acirema, combined with the dark skin of his grandmother and the commanding voice of his father. When he laughs the Tupi hear a happy child, and Acirema hears Zumbi's laughter echoing through all those years and across all those distances—especially when the full moon illuminates the night sky. On those nights she cries on her mother's shoulder after putting Kauan to sleep.

One day Zuleika says to her, "The Portuguese have a word for this: *saudade.* It is the profound sadness of missing something we love when we secretly know we cannot have it back."

"How do I get over it?"

"You don't. I have *saudade* from Africa. There are days, when the rays of the sun cut through the leaves in a certain way, that deep in my soul I see the African forest again. It hurts. I know it will pass, as much as I know it will come back again. It is part of my life, my history. I remind myself that I have Tuibae, that I found in this forsaken land love in the arms of an old blind Tupi man, that this love brought me you, and that you generated Kauan. I am happy with tears. That is life."

***

Zumbi's *Saudade*, or What One Learns with Peasants

In Palmares Zumbi also goes through the pain of *saudade.* Many a day he spends so much time away from his classmates and batchmates, they keep asking themselves where he is and what he is doing—and more importantly, with whom. They believe the answer may be juicy gossip.

The true answer is that most of his hours out of school are spent in the woods and streams, alone with his memories of Acirema and only Pintada by his side. The jaguar seems to feel his deep-seated pain and sorrow; she just lies by him and purrs, like the huge cat she is. The other way he passes time is working with farmers and cattle ranchers, the work distracting from his sadness and longing. Since telling others he is spending so much time alone in the woods will draw suspicion and disbelief, when asked about his whereabouts he tells them about his time with the farmers and ranchers.

"Farmers and ranchers? Peasants? Why would you waste your time with such people?" they ask him.

"I enjoy and I learn a lot from them, you know" Zumbi says.

"What does one learn from farmers and ranchers?"

Zumbi smiles and tries to move on. They insist.

"Come on, tell us what you learn from these ignorant old folks in fields and farms?"

It is irritating to hear such provocations and Zumbi is not impervious to that irritation.

"Here is what I learn: if you plant oranges you get oranges, and if you plant beans you get beans." His friends look at each other with smirks, so Zumbi continues. "No matter how much manure you put on the soil, there is no way you will get oranges out of beanstalks or beans out of orange trees. The treatment of the soil is important, for the orange trees may be strong and fruitful or weak and bare. But it will always yield oranges. So, Antonio, I look at people now, and at myself, and think: Is this an orange or a bean or a papaya?

Because you cannot help but be who you are. You my friend, are my friend, so please let me be."

He walks out alone, Pintada by his side, and his class-mates laugh and joke while Antonio remains serious, thinking about oranges, and beans, and papayas, and people.

Russian Interlude: 1672

The prince is born in the summertime, a good auspice in a place where winters are brutal and unforgiving. In time he too will be occasionally brutal and unforgiving, but now he is said to have good health, his mother's black, vaguely Tatar eyes, and a tuft of auburn hair. He will keep that sunny disposition and inherit a throne despite other heirs born ahead of him. They are sickly while he is not.

At age ten he will be named Tsar with his mother as the regent, and they will rule over a nation bigger than an ocean. His pastimes include sailing and shipbuilding, and as ruler he will build his country a navy. He will also move his court closer to the sea and build a magnificent city that will bear his name. In order to find those ports, he will fight the Turks in the South and the Swedes in the North. In order to find peace, he will kill his own kin.

He will grow as large as his country and stand head and shoulders over most of Europe at six feet eight. He is a giant of a man, ruling over a slumbering giant of a country that will shake the world when it wakes up.

His title is the most excellent and great sovereign prince, the ruler of all the Russias: of Moscow, of Kiev, of Vladimir, of Novgorod, Tsar of Kazan, Tsar of Astrakhan and Tsar of Siberia, sovereign of Pskov, great prince of Smolensk, of Tver, of Yugorsk, of Perm, of Vyatka, of Bulgaria and others, sovereign and great prince of the Novgorod Lower lands, of Chernigov, of Ryazan, of Rostov, of Yaroslavl, of Belozersk, of Udora, of Kondia and the sovereign of all the northern lands, and the sovereign of the Iverian lands, of the Kartlian and Georgian Kings, of the Kabardin lands, of the Circassian and Mountain princes and many other states and lands western and eastern here and there and the successor and sovereign and ruler.

His name is Pyotr Alekseyevich Romanov. He is remembered as Peter the Great.

CHAPTER 12

ROYAL WEDDINGS

1675

For those who rule, marriage is a business, a result of convoluted political and diplomatic negotiations. King Ganga Zumba now has two princes turning twenty years of age, and his calculations are worthy of Master Yalom's quadrivium test. In his royal estimation, both Andala and Zumbi are ready to make him allies before making Palmares heirs.

There are two villages whose chiefs have young daughters at marriageable age: Zambi and Osenga. These are two villages surrounding citadels that flank Palmares to the east and west, both growing in population and importance—and both in need of closer ties with the central authority at the Macaco. Osenga is bigger, bordering the land of the Tupi, and Ganga Zumba plans to have his own son Andala seal that alliance. He knows Andala will follow his command and hopes Zumbi will follow as easily. Since his decision to prohibit Zumbi's relationship with Acirema, their relations have turned cold and distant.

The three boys—Zumbi, Andala, and Antonio Soares—are the senior class of the boy's hut. While they are still very close, Andala and Antonio are always running boys' games while Zumbi keeps more to himself. Ever since he'd had the enchanted nights with Yara and the aching loss of Acirema, which remain private, painful, and powerful memories to him, Zumbi is very reserved. Ever since those recollections lodged in his soul and his history, he has preferred solitude and quiet spaces, spending long periods alone with Pintada in the woods, revisiting places where he was once happy with Acirema.

By now, Ganga Zumba has forgotten about Acirema's story and he is grateful that Zumbi does not appear to dwell on, in public, or hold grudges, in private, about his royal order. He brings in the chiefs of both villages and proposes marriage to solidify their confederation. The chiefs come with their families, Chiamaka's from Zambi and Ashon's from Osenga. The moment Dandara, Chief Chiamaka's only daughter, enters the room, all elders fall silent.

Dandara is now a very tall, slim African teen, only fifteen years of age. Her beauty, grace, and allure are legendary around the villages and her father Chiamaka is very protective of her. She is receiving lectures at home so that she does not have to leave her hometown of Zambi.

Ashon of the Osenga house brings his daughter, Binty, whose physical presence is not as powerful as Dandara's but whose personality is strong and domineering. Binty and Andala's wedding arrangement is easy and straightforward, as they both were raised pleasing and being pleased by their fathers. Binty herself is determined to join the most royal family of Palmares.

Zumbi's strained relationship to Ganga Zumbi and Dandara's steely personality make their arrangement more tentative.

Ganga Zumbi invites the princes to join the councilmen and the visiting families. Zumbi is still nursing the pain and grief inside his soul. At night he alternates between making plans about running away and finding Acirema and musing about joining the circus of Albion and going around the world with Yara. He has no peace and little patience for boys' games. The only solace he finds is in study and work. Zumbi loves to farm with the other working men and also enjoys hunting and fishing mostly alone with Pintada. In the fields he joins the farmers and cowboys. These are older men, but he finds their serious dedication to work more bearable than the boys' enthusiasm for girls and games. And so it is through pain and suffering that he has aged faster than the other teens.

They know Ganga Zumba is negotiating alliances and political deals and they know the part they have to play. Zumbi does not believe anything can change his mind about staying a recluse, maybe even becoming a monk or a marabout. He loses himself in thought at times thinking about Yara or Acirema; he keeps remembering the sea and the beach and wondering about the Tupi lands in the distance.

Yet he knows they are gone. There are moving on with their lives on this planet full of forgetfulness and neglect. He is the one who is stuck and, worse yet, wants to be stuck. He fights to keep the memory of their faces, their smells, the sound of their laughter with him all days and, more importantly, all nights. Some questions keep haunting his mind: What else is out there in the world but suffering? Who else is out there in the world but fools? What else is there to do but wait for death?

But now all those questions and all his daydreams and musings halt the moment Zumbi's eyes settle on Dandara of the Zambi village. The vision of this African young woman—her beautiful face above her long neck, her large dark piercing eyes, her delicate shoulders and firm chest, her long, strong legs on which she stands tall—is the instant cure to his long sickness.

There are many stories told about the ends of marriages, about how they wither and collapse in divorce or death. As many stories remain untold about the beginnings of marriages, about how they sprout out of love and hope. There are many stories told about romantic marriages, about how two lovers fight the world against all odds for their own infatuation. As many stories remain untold about arranged marriages, about how the wisdom and patience of elders who match young bodies produces many a happy couple. This is the story of the beginning of a happy arranged marriage.

Dandara is a princess of her tribe and her father has agreed no wedding is happening until she agrees on the choice of her partner. Like all in Palmares, she has heard of the orphan prince and like many in Palmares, she admires his humble presence and his leading role in the conquest of Garanhuns. Yet she asks to have a walk with him before agreeing on her father's dealing with Ganga Zumba. The court awaits this fateful conversation between the twenty-year-old prince and the stunning fifteen-year-old princess.

And so they go to the orchard behind the royal palace, a place full of tropical trees including oranges, avocados, mangos, *siriguelas*, guavas, and several palms. These plants are silent witness to many secret deals and diplomatic agreements that keep a community united under constant attack.

"They were all looking at us," says Zumbi.

"You should be used to that by now," says Dandara, still looking straight ahead.

"Maybe it was strange because this time they were actually all looking only at you."

"I am fine with the looking. Now they are all talking about us. I am used to that too."

"So, what should we talk about?"

"Us."

Zumbi, who is finally overcoming the mesmerizing effect of her beauty, is now in awe of her intelligence and keen mind. At this moment it feels like talking to her takes more courage than attacking Garanhuns, but he continues:

"Before we talk about us, I need to tell you about me."

The tentative pair sits under a large mango tree and he tells her all about Acirema and Yara. He talks about Yara and how she taught him gently the art of loving with one's whole body, not only with eyes and hands. After that, he has mustered enough courage to tell her about his child, who he believes is growing up on Tupi lands, and how he dreams about them constantly. She is the first one to hear about his big shame. Dandara listens quietly and seriously to each word, nodding at times. At the conclusion of his tales, Zumbi looks at Dandara and seriously adds, "I understand if you prefer not to join me in marriage."

She takes her time before speaking. A long silence falls between them. Finally, she holds his large hands stares into his watered eyes and speaks.

"Your past is in the past. There is no way of changing it. This is your life, your history. What we can change is the future. You need to make a promise that those two women were your first and last adventures. As for the child, it is your child, and I will love my husband's child. Not like my own, but I will love the child."

Zumbi listens to each word. She then adds, for the first time coy, "As for your learning about loving with your body, one of us had better know what to do when it comes time for that."

Zumbi is taken by her straightforward language, her matter-of-fact attitude. She has certainly grown up in a family used to ruling others, for before you rule others you learn to rule your own mind. He falls to his knees and promises, "Dandara, Princess of Zambi, I ask you to take me as your husband and I promise to love and respect you till death set us apart."

She helps him up and they embrace tightly for the first time, thus transforming an arranged marriage into a romantic choice and lifelong pact of partnership.

All eyes are on the couple as they walk back into the royal palace, but it does not matter to them anymore. Andala and Binty are waiting, for theirs was a quick decision. By the way Dandara and Zumbi walk back into the palace, it is obvious to anyone watching that they are now a couple as well.

Ganga Zumba and Chiamaka look at each other and nod. The king embraces his nephew and with tear in his eye whispers in his ear "Your mother Sabina is happy and she is here with us today." Chiamaka embraces his daughter and signals her mother to join them. Doriana brings the four elements to the two couples and explains their meaning.

"For this ceremony, the couple gets a taste of four flavors meant to represent the distinct stages within a marriage: cayenne for spiciness, lemon for sourness, vinegar for bitterness, and honey for sweetness."

They taste them together, the people around them clapping at each flavor, amused by their reactions.

Master Yalom steps in and reads a Talmud passage.

Blessed art though, O Lord, King of the Universe, who created mirth and joy, bridegroom and bride, gladness, jubilation, dancing, and delight, love and brotherhood, peace and fellowship. Quickly, O Lord our God, may the sound of mirth and joy be heard in the streets of Judah and Jerusalem, the voice of bridegroom and bride, jubilant voices of bridegrooms from their canopies and youths from the feasts of song. Blessed art though, O Lord, who makes the bridegroom rejoice with the bride.

The Catholic priest comes and reads a passage from the Song of Solomon.

I am my beloved's and my beloved is mine.

My beloved speaks and says to me: Arise, my love, my fair one, and come away; for lo, the winter is past, the rain is over and gone. The flowers appear on the earth, the time of singing has come, and the voice of the turtledove is heard in our land. The fig tree puts forth its figs, and the vines are in blossom; they give forth fragrance.

Arise, my love, my fair one, and come away. I am my beloved's and my beloved is mine. O my dove, in the clefts of the rock, in the covert of the cliff, let me see your face, let me hear your voice, for your voice is sweet, and your face is comely. Set me as a seal upon your heart and seal upon your arm; for love is strong as death, jealousy cruel as the grave.

The Iman comes and gives his blessing.

> *Oh Allah, bless our marriage and let it be a means for us to become closer to You in love and devotion. Let it be a source of untold blessings, happiness and joy.*
>
> *Oh Allah, let our marriage be a way for us and our families to enter Jannah.*
>
> *Ya Allah, protect our marriage from the whisperings of Shaytan. Give us the strength to live together in justice, equity, love and, mercy.*
>
> *My Lord, let this marriage bring untold blessings to us individually, to our families, and our children In-sha Allah.*
>
> *My Creator, bless us with children who will be a source of great joy and happiness.*
>
> *Oh Allah, give us the love which you had blessed Muhammad, Allah's Peace and blessings be upon him, and Khadija with, May Allah be pleased with her.*

On hearing this, Dandara raises her hand and everyone is quiet. Taking Zumbi's hands and looking him straight in the eye, she completes the blessings.

> *Grow old along with me!*
> *The best is yet to be,*
> *The last of life, for which the first was made,*
> *Our times are in His hand*
> *Who saith "A whole I planned,*
> *"Youth shows but half; trust God:*
> *See all, nor be afraid!"*

All traditions speaking similar wishes and requesting similar protection, using the many different names given to God.

And so Zumbi and Andala are wed that same night into different families of other villages. This is an age of practical people, even for the royals. Ganga Zumba orders a community banquet, and the cooks and maids get to work. Now the ambrosial scents come not from the orchard but from the kitchens where papayas, bananas, pineapples, mangos, *siriguelas*, guavas, and oranges are the raw material for desserts and where chicken, corn, and fish grill. At the banquet, Wonder presents a song about love he calls "Overjoy" in which he tells them *All true love needs is a chance.*

And they found that chance or chance found them, two royal lines of African blood merging in the tropical soil of lands that one day will be known as Brazil.

***

The next day they depart, Zumbi to the village of Zambi with Dandara's family, and Andala to Osenga with Binty and her family. The people of Macaco, especially those in the royal compound, are saddened by the departure of their young princes but know their role in keeping Palmares united. Life goes on, as it has to. They are doing the job only they can do; as Queen Aqualtune used to say, they are "making themselves useful."

At Zambi the ruler's hut is a smaller version of the royal palace in Macaco, also done in Bantu style. Dandara and Zumbi now occupy a wing of the compound. Pintada gets used to the new place before the people of Zambi get used to her.

153

Zumbi takes time to get to know his new village and he enjoys his new family. At times his old reminiscences appear to him in dreams but as soon as he sees the beautiful Dandara by his side, his heart settles down. Soon they have their first child, a girl they name Cilene. The birth is uncomplicated but Zumbi is very nervous, haunted by the stories he has heard and what his imagination made of how his mother died.

When the baby girl is brought to him Zumbi takes her in his powerful arms, ever so careful, and dances with her, singing to her one of Wonder's songs, "For once in my life." At that moment, looking at his daughter's eyes, Zumbi understands the full meaning of that song. The new hope of a new life, another line of destiny beginning its way in the world. Even the usually stern Chiamaka smiles and laughs with his grandchild. Her name is Cilene but everyone calls her "Little Queen." The same spell Dandara once placed on Chiamaka, now Cilene places on Zumbi.

Each of the following two years brings a new child. The second-born is a boy named Felix and the third another boy, to be called Umbelino. In the span of three happy years Zumbi goes from having Pintada as his only companion to having Dandara, Cilene, Felix, and Umbelino. With Chiamaka, they are the ruling family of Zambi, and what they have in abundance is love. Love between Zumbi and Dandara as parents, love between them and their children.

In these days Zumbi spends his time between hunting with Pintada and one of the children, practicing capoeira and weapons with the guard, managing the village with his father-in-law Chiamaka, and reading his favorite books from the days of the trivium to the children. About once a month he goes with Chiamaka to Macaco for the royal council and has a chance to meet Andala and Antonio Soares. Though different as adults they share enough childhood memories to remain close. At the end of the day and of each task what he looks forward to is Dandara's embrace and his children's smiles as they watch him coming back to them. From time to time Zumbi remembers Doriana's words: silence at the front means the Portuguese are planning something.

Yet these are three years of love. If only the world would let love rest.

Indian Interlude: Delhi, 1675

He is now fifty-four years of age and is under arrest by the Muslim authorities of the Mughal Empire for resisting forced conversion of Hindus and Sikhs to Islam.

Eleven years before he had become the ninth Sikh Guru after the faithful had heard the last instructions of their former guru as *Baba Bakala*, meaning his successor was to be found in the city of Bakala. Following that prophesy several claimants to the title moved to the city. A wealthy merchant named Baba Makhan Shah Labana had once prayed for his life and had promised to gift five hundred gold coins to the Sikh Guru if he survived. He then arrived in Bakala only to find nine men claiming the title of Sikh Guru.

The word Guru itself is thought to have two roots, *Gu* meaning darkness and *Ru* meaning light, making *guru* one who brings light into darkness. The merchant Baba Labana sought to bring light into the obscure dispute and went around distributing two gold coins to the different claimants, who promptly accepted the gift. When he came to our character, the merchant was told his two coins were quite short of the promised five hundred coins. The merchant then ran to the rooftop and shouted, "I have found the Guru, I have found the Guru!"

As Sikh Guru he travelled extensively, preached, and wrote many tracts on the nature of God, of human attachments, about body, mind, sorrow, dignity, service, death, and deliverance. He also supported the people in their resistance to abandoning the faith of their forefathers.

He appointed his son as the next Sikh Guru and entered the city of Ropar, where he was promptly placed under arrest to be transferred to Delhi in November. There, he was asked to perform a miracle to prove his closeness to God. He refused. One more time, he was asked to convert to Islam. One more time, he refused.

Now, on the twenty-fourth of November, 1675, he is executed for his refusal at Chandni Chowk, in what is today Delhi.

He is remembered as the ninth Sikh Guru and his name is Tegh Bahadur.

CHAPTER 13

THE END OF INNOCENCE

1677

The conquest of Garanhuns in 1670 marks a high point in Palmares' expansion and power, and this makes the Portuguese very nervous. Several punitive expeditions are sent but are promptly repelled by the African forces. A puzzle continues to swirl among the Portuguese settlers: How can these slaves resist troops armed with European muskets and solid Iberian steel? The Portuguese governor's worst nightmare is now whispered across Recife as a frightening question: Are the Africans developing their own steel weapons?

In Palmares, the people are happy and confident. The royal family is flourishing. Prince Zumbi, now known as Zumbi of Zambi, is coming of age strong and prosperous, and so is the quilombo. In each of the now six citadels, a familiar sound is starting to echo: the sound of blacksmiths working, hitting their anvils with decision and craft, creating hoes, knives, machetes, axes and hatchets, and arrowheads and swords. Expeditions ordered by Ganga Zumba, and guided by Tupi, found generous deposits of hematite, which is now mined and smelted into iron to be forged into steel in the heart of the forest.

The Portuguese governor in Recife hears of one Fernão Carrilho, a ruthless, brutal, and intemperate mercenary. He once attacked some quilombos near Bahia, and when his own men deserted him he recruited Native troops, attacking the villages where two hundred lived and bringing twenty back alive in chains. On a second attack, again his own troops left him in the battlefield. He persisted with one man left on his side and destroyed another village, bringing back twelve alive and not bothering to count the dead this time.

"That is the man we need to take care of Palmares," concludes the governor of Pernambuco.

The Portuguese bring Carrilho to Recife and give him the rank of Captain Major in their army. He asks for four hundred men; they give him one hundred and eighty-five including some Tupi troops. He knows he does not have numbers, only a chance to kill a few and make some money selling the survivors. He is not a man to pass on such a chance.

The march toward Palmares is reluctant but proceeds. As the distance from the coast increases, the mountains start to stare at them from the peaks—every sunset casting long shadows over their march. One of his lieutenants approaches him with concerns.

"Sire, the men are nervous. We are not even two hundred and we are marching uphill against thousands."

"We are White, they are Black. We are born to rule and command. They are born to obey and kneel."

The lieutenant looks around at their native troops, take stock of their firepower, and continues to worry.

Departing Porto Calvo, the river and the mountain ridges take Carrilho troops northwest. Every night the men again talk about going back to the coast. Every night, Carrilho continues his diatribes.

"They are slaves, we are their owners. They will see us and surrender. It is their nature."

It is now October and they have been walking for thirteen straight days. The speeches start to repeat themselves, the pompous phrases and disdain for Africans only increasing at each iteration.

As they move, the mountains topped with palm trees loom in the horizon, closer and closer.

"When you see the palm trees, the palm trees see you," says one of Carrilho's men.

On the fourteenth day thy stumble into a group of houses, the families surprised in their daily routine. These are people who live off their land, small farmer families. These are not warriors; they are mostly unarmed for they live in peace.

Carrilho orders a line of muskets and they fire at his command. The many shots sound together like one large explosion. This opening salvo has two effects.

The first effect is that it sounds the alarm to all families in the surrounding area. They flee. Having practiced the ways and paths of the nearby forest, they disappear instantly. Women and children are the first to go, with them their animals. The few men stay behind to protect the retreat of the women and children with machetes and axes. Even some of the men have time to escape as the troops recharge their muskets.

The second effect is that it spreads death. The men, women, and children caught by that first firing—taken without warning, no chance to surrender—fall dead on the spot. They do not see their killers, do not look their executioners in the eye. Their instant death is announced by the noise of muskets and a sudden pain. They were waking up and checking their chickens, they were tending their gardens, now they are dead.

Carrilho and his men advance, yelling and celebrating. All they find are corpses and silence. Except for those loved ones who could not leave their family dead behind and stay holding their bodies, tears of despair and pain running down their faces. They are met with no mercy, no compassion. They are taken prisoners. Back to slavery. Many do not care, now that their mothers, fathers, and children are dead. Life is gone. These children, who have so far only experienced peace and love, and now bound to face the horror and hate of slavery.

From a settlement of a few hundred Africans, Carrilho takes ten prisoners, kills fifteen, and misses the others to the forest. The troops set fire to the huts and houses. He wants to know where they will run to now, where the next village is?

There is only one way to know: interrogate the prisoners, which is work for the next morning when the prisoners are hungry, afraid, and no longer in shock. They spend the night in the rubble of their own burning homes.

"How can I interrogate them without torture since I cannot risk mangling an able body?" That is the question Carrilho goes to sleep with.

The morning comes. The prisoners are hungry, scared, and mourning their loved ones. They are separated from each other so not even the consolation of their shared pain is allowed. Each spent the night alone with their own tears.

Carrilho starts with the women. They do not say anything despite his threats and their fear. Their tears are all he gets. The children are not much use, except that he remembers one of them was captured in the arms of one of the men. Father and son hunching over the dead body of the mother. There are only two men among the captured; they are now Carrilho's last hope for information and they also will get him the most money on the slave market.

"Do you ever want to see your daughter alive again?"

The man is named Kasim and his daughter Anisa is held in the next room. He can only hear her screams. Carrilho looks at him and repeats.

"Do you ever want to see your daughter alive again?"

Once again, silence is the only response he gets. In a fit of anger, not entirely insincere, he takes out a leather whip and shows it to Kasim. Carrilho leaves the room and repeats the question:

"Do you ever want to see your daughter alive again?"

Kasim's silence is responded to by an order.

"Strike!"

From the other room the whip's sound cutting the air is followed by Anisa's scream. She is eight years old and she is scared. Kasim tries to stand up but his hands are tied behind his back and powerful arms push him back in the seat.

"Do you ever want to see your daughter alive again?"

"Yes. Please stop."

"That man outside the room, holding my whip, has your daughter with him. She called for you many times. She even said her papa's name ... Kasim!"

Kasim looks at him with exhausted fury. Carrilho continues to talk.

"The whip they are using, it is fit for oxen and horses."

"She is eight years old!" Kasim whispers, letting go thick tears that run down his prominent cheekbones.

"Ah! You can speak! Now that we have established that, you will tell me what I need to know."

"Just stop hitting her."

"The hitting stops when you start talking."

"What do you want to know?"

Carrilho smiles for the first time. His eyes are beaming with the prospect of a straight path toward the heart of Palmares.

"It is actually a very simple question to which you have the answer. Where is the next village?"

Kasim tears do not stop as he thinks about his people, the many pathways in the forest, the nights together as one family.

"Subupira is next. That is where you will die."

"Subupira? North? South? West?"

"Two-day walk, with the setting sun on your right side."

"That makes it south. Subupira, how many families?"

"They say one thousand."

"That is at least five thousand people." Carrilho's brain starts to calculate how much money such prey would fetch. Enough to make him a damn rich man. He recounts his own troops and tries to convince himself they can win this attack. He does the math time and again, each time getting more confident of their superior in power despite much inferior numbers.

The afternoon is spent in preparation, with the main decision being what to do with the prisoners. Carrilho's lieutenant Alvin favors executing them all and leaving them hanging as a warning to others. Carrilho himself, always the businessman, sees this savage strategy as monetary foolery. He sends the ten captives with a small escort back to Porto Calvo and from there to Recife. His instructions include clear directions to keep the families apart.

***

At that very moment in the royal compound in Macaco, Ganga Zumba is meeting with his main advisors. The ears and eyes of the forest have alerted them to the attack the day before. The king is worried, the council divided. Zumbi, now leader in the village of Zambi, and prince Andala, leader in Osenga, are brought in along with the leader of each citadel. The Moor is there, quiet as usual. They are considering all options.

"Maybe this is the result of the attack on Garanhuns."

"This is a meeting to discuss not the causes but the solutions," intervenes Doriana.

The Moor nods and speaks, with his usual authority and military mind. "The Portuguese cannot strike back from the north or west, so they will find the soft spot coming from the east, the coast, where they are strong. Gaining the foothold in Garanhuns was correct."

Zumbi listens, the talkative boy now a pensive man, aware of the cause and effect of each movement, weary of the brutal reality of power, war, and slavery.

Someone volunteers to speak what is on everyone's minds. "We can retreat."

Silence falls again like a blanket or a fog. Zumbi considers his words and finally speaks. "The logical conclusion of a strategy of retreating is defeat."

Ganga Zumba looks at his nephew and wishes his son would possess that same mix of courage and wisdom. As if sensing the need to speak, Prince Andala counters.

"But retreating now will allow us to save the people of Subupira and prepare a strong resistance back here at the Macaco."

Several heads now shake in disbelief. Retreat to one's capital is a risky move, sometimes deadly, most times desperate. Doriana asks an open question to all in the room.

"What is the message we give by retreating?"

"That we are afraid," volunteers one voice.

"That we are weak," says another.

"What else?" she incites them.

"That we are out of ammunition," adds another voice.

Doriana looks at the Moor and recognizes the new insight in his stare.

"Retreating a fortress like Subupira also sends the message that we have more fortifications that are even more powerful hidden in the forest."

Silence returns to the room, but now with a shade of hope. Zumbi breaks the silence.

"So, retreating can show strength instead of weakness?"

As a teacher, Doriana cannot help but assume the professorial tone.

"If we leave Subupira as if that is just another fortification to be abandoned at the first sign of danger, the Portuguese will realize we have much more waiting for them in the forest. They will take this message back to Recife. They will themselves retreat back to the coast."

Ganga Zumba is ready now, having heard enough.

"Time is needed to organize such a move. We are retreating, but not to Macaco. I am not taking refugees from my own people in our capital. I want to have the families of Subupira resettled. Zumbi, you take two hundred families to Zambi and two hundred to Garanhuns. Andala, take four hundred to Osenga. The rest will go to Amaro."

The decision is made. Execution is pressing. It is now a race against Carrilho's advance.

The room is quiet for a few more minutes. Ganga Zumba concludes the meeting.

"Start!" orders the king and as everyone is still under the spell of the moment he lets out a direct command: "Now!"

Everyone leaves but Doriana, Hermes, and the Moor.

***

Carrilho moves toward Subupira as fast as he can. On his way he crosses a few orchards and small plantations that grow timidly under the tropical sun. He has them burned to the ground.

After a few days he sees it. Subupira has a tall palisade made of palm tree trunks. The men are impressed by its majestic position on top of a hill. They prepare for arrows that never come. Cautiously, they move into the town. A few traps are left and men fall into them, none getting hurt but all getting angry. Carrilho waits outside with a contingent and eventually is called in. What he finds is silence and destruction. The citadel is burned before his eyes.

He walks around, sees the burned remains of a Catholic church, the huts where children were educated. He sees the center compound with its solid foundation. Fire can destroy structures, but traces of careful craftsmanship are visible in the rubble.

Carrilho sees the center square, sees the marketplace, sees the many streets and the marks of cattle, people, and chickens, sees a once beautiful and proud city. He examines the palisade and walks up its walls. The views from the top are impressive. From this vantage point the city defenders could have inflicted a shower of arrows over them. They could have spotted them a day before.

As he muses about these facts his men call him to show him an ominous sight: left among the burned remains of a workshop are two brand new swords, made of the most reinforced steel. Two new swords that could have only been made right there, at the heart of Subupira. The whispered nightmare of the Portuguese that started as a question now has a clear and shining answer: the Africans are developing their own steel weapons.

The Africans can now make steel better than the Portuguese can in the New World. Carrilho goes to sleep that night in order to escape his worst nightmare.

And so, lessons are learned among both peoples and innocence is lost once again. News flies fast. The Portuguese learn about Palmares' military architecture, staring in awe of the descriptions of Subupira's walls, size, and buildings. The Africans learn about the infinite supply of weapons, men, and cruelty available to the Portuguese. Both sides face the choice between a hurriedly arranged peace or a long, bloody, and violent war of mutual destruction.

American Interlude: Massachusetts Bay and Rhode Island Colonies, 1676

He dreams of uniting all native tribes—Wampnoag, Narragansett, Nipmuck, Pequot, and Mohegan—against these pale strangers known as Puritans. One day he starts conceiving attack plans to contain their ever-stronger push.

In 1663 these colonists had published, at the Harvard College in Cambridge, their most powerful weapon and most dangerous of books: the complete Bible in the Algonquin language, to be known as The *Eliot Indian Bible*. One of his own tribesmen, John Sassamon, converted not only to their religion but to their cause, and betrays his secrets, plans, and intentions to the Puritan authorities.

He orders Sassamon's execution. The Puritans in turn execute the executioners. This opens the cycle of murder and revenge we know as war.

Boston and Plymouth prepare their troops and he prepares his many forces. The first attack is on the colonial settlement of Swansea, prompting the New England Confederation to declare war on him. At the Battle of Bloody Brook, the colonial troops are beaten. Taking the offensive, native troops attack, overrun, and burn Springfield, Massachusetts. Among many victories and raids, the one defeat is the Great Swamp Fight around Christmastime. They push and finally attack Plymouth as well as Providence, Rhode Island, which is left burned.

The tide eventually turns now, in the summer of 1676, one century before the nation breaks from British royal rule. The native tribes' confederation crumbles and falls. Among the colonial troops are a number of converted natives. Among them there is a man who has taken the name John Alderman. This man is the one who takes aim, fires, and shoots our character dead in battle. His head will be displayed for the next twenty years atop Burial Hill in Plymouth, a warning and a reminder to natives and colonists.

The dream of an American independence away from European colonists fades. These and other drafts of natives' dreams will be related by Increase Mather as *Relation of the Troubles Which Have Happened in New England*, in which he argues for the "wonderful providence of God in disappointing their devices."

He has become known as King Philip, a Native American king, and that is how this war will be remembered and then forgotten: King Philip's War.

His name is Metacomet.

CHAPTER 14

GANGA ZUMBA VISITS RECIFE

1678

Recife has been a Portuguese city again now for twenty-four years, after a generation as the capital of the Dutch sugar empire. Here the first synagogue in the Americas is built and here men and women from Africa are traded on the evilest market. Recife is a global city in the 1600s and as one of the world's commercial hubs, it cannot escape the disgrace of its age. It is from here that settlers will migrate and help create the village of New Amsterdam, eventually to be renamed New York City.

In these eight years since the fall of Garanhuns, the Portuguese have kept to themselves and tried to ignore the flourishing African kingdom next to them. The flow of enslaved men and women continue from Angola, providing ample supply of strong arms for the sugarcane plantations. The province remains the top sugar-production region in the world.

A clear message of compromise needs to be sent to Palmares, and the heart of this message is the messenger. Those negotiations will require courage to compromise on both sides. None is ready for it—until they are.

Captain Antonio Pinto Pereira, a Black man, comes alone. An officer from the Black regiment of Henrique Dias, the same Black regiment that helped expel the Dutch occupiers, he comes to Palmares and asks to speak to its leader. Since he is Black, he is brought straight to Ganga Zumba and the council at the center of Macaco. The beauty and strength of the fortifications send their own message to the messenger.

He does not kneel in front of the king but bows in respect.

"Captain, you are welcome in our community," says Ganga Zumba.

"Lord Ganga Zumba, the Portuguese are organizing another expedition under Carrilho, with more men and better weapons."

"That is not a real threat. It would be if they were sending better men and more weapons," says Zumbi, breaking the ice in the room.

"He already destroyed Subupira, Lord Ganga Zumba," replies Captain Pereira, ignoring the joke.

"They did not destroy it—we did," interjects the Moor who is impatiently standing in a corner. "We call it 'scorched earth' strategy. During these attacks, our troops will destroy valuable goods—crops, buildings, routes in and out of towns—in order to make them unusable by enemy troops. The enemy will starve in our fertile land and fields. You are the enemy."

Captain Pereira looks at the stern presence of the Moor with a deep sadness, the sadness of one who forgot his own people and can barely recognize himself.

"Lord Ganga Zumba, what is better for your people: war or peace?"

Zumbi and the Moor want to respond but Ganga Zumba raises his hand, silencing them.

"Peace is better. Peace with freedom," he says.

Captain Pereira finds the opening he needs.

"Sir, the governor of Pernambuco is extending a peace offer to you."

That sentence is followed by silence. Silence that follows an utterance heard for the first. Silence of opening vistas, silence of new possibilities—possibilities that until then were impossibilities. What is unheard is impossible; what is now spoken transforms into different possibilities in each mind in the room.

"Please stay the night, Captain. We will meet again tomorrow. You may leave now."

The council is again united in disagreement. Doriana, the Moor, and Zumbi are skeptical of the Portuguese's motives and words; Andala, Antonio Soares, and Ganga Zona want to consider the offer. Hermes is quiet listening to each argument. The king, Ganga Zumba, does not take sides.

"Peace is the only option. We need to find a way to live side by side with them."

"Maybe you can negotiate a way back to Africa."

"The pale hands will never extend a hand to the Black hands unless they have to do so. They are weak now. Let us attack instead."

"We can unite Palmares and the Tupi nation and drive the Portuguese to sea."

"We can negotiate property of land and we will become farmers and ranchers. We will beat them at their own game."

"The only way we will survive is by accommodating."

"They will never conquer Palmares unless we surrender. Accepting a peace offer by those who enslave us is surrendering."

"Palmares has flourished for seventy-five years. We are prospering without them—what do we need them for? Why now?"

"Do you call this flourishing? We just burned our own city of Subupira!"

"They will never abide by an agreement signed by a Black hand."

"The same way we captured Garanhuns, we can organize a counter expedition and attack Porto Calvo, then one day Recife."

"We know these mountains and forests better than the Portuguese know the ocean. We will defend our borders; they will stay on the coast."

The discussion enters the night and the people notice their leaders absent from their community dinner. Ganga Zumba orders the Catholic priest, the Iman, and the high-priest of African gods to hold services for wisdom. As the night grows cold, the argument heats up. It is past midnight when they retire, and even then the groups continue side conversations in whispers through the night.

In the morning Ganga Zumba goes to mass. Most of the community is present. The priest, aware of the rumors, partially aware of the discussions, prepares a long sermon for the success of Palmares armies against Portugal. The community is ready and eager to listen as he is known for wisdom and courage, a rare combination among priests. The last words of his sermon echo through the community and the morning.

If this is the reward for our travails, why did we toil so hard? Why so much blood and so much fight? Why did we escape into the night, toward woods and forests unknown? Why did we lay the foundations of a city on the hill? If this is the reward, let us leave behind the ferocious sign of Leo and step forward toward the sign of Virgo, kind and benevolent. Forgive us, Lord, by the merits of the virgin and if she intercedes for our forgiveness, as a mother she requests and receives. And if you forgive us we can others forgive, in the name of your unending love.

The sermon's words have a profound and strange effect on those hearing it: each leaves believing the words justified their positions. Those against peace are now more opposed to any agreement, and those for an agreement are convinced peace is the only option ahead.

Ganga Zumba reconvenes his cabinet after the service. They walk in, each with his own thoughts, looking at a king who has aged overnight. His voice is still commanding, yet now the fighting spirit is no longer present. He calls for no discussion and sends for Captain Pereira.

"I have reached my decision."

Nobody speaks, as too many words have been used already despite both sides still believing not enough was said.

"A leader must make decisions based on imperfect and incomplete information. We have been at war with the Portuguese for more than seventy-five years. We now have a generation born in Palmares who do not understand what it is like to live under the whip of a master. I am happy that they have known love and kindness, not the brutal violence of enslavement.

"This generation will beget another generation and that another. Each generation born and raised in freedom is a promise to the future, that one day Portuguese and Africans will sit together at the same table as children of the same god, may we call him Jesus, Allah, or Olodumare. We need to save Palmares for that generation to grow, prosper, and bring us the next generation, bigger, stronger, wealthier."

The words flow, and as with the sermon, each party reads into it a justification for yes or for no. The concluding words, however, are again ominous.

"I am sending a delegation back to Recife to negotiate with the Portuguese."

Zumbi, the Moor, and Doriana wait for the names in the delegation, as that choice will determine the outcome of the negotiations.

"My brother Ganga Zona and my son Andala will return with Captain Pereira and bring us the negotiated terms. The final word will be mine."

Zumbi interjects. "My lord—"

"Only those open to negotiations can negotiate. They shall go."

"Uncle—"

"Silence! The decision is made, you must do as you are told. You all must do as you are told!"

A lonely tear runs down Doriana's face. The Moor, a military man used to obeying, lowers his gaze. Zumbi storms out of the room with Pintada.

***

A Visit to Recife

Ganga Zona and Prince Andala go to Recife to start negotiations, serving as delegates for King Ganga Zumba. The Portuguese governor himself is a delegate for the King of Portugal. They meet and discuss potential terms. The Portuguese invite Ganga Zona and Andala to attend mass. They provide them with gifts of clothes that the men from Palmares notice are not as well cut as the ones they have. They return to Palmares with secret papers, and similar secret manuscripts are sent from Recife to Lisbon. The kings should decide. Letters follow, from Palmares to Recife, from Recife to Lisbon, and back.

Ganga Zumba now spends his days debating with others and his nights debating with himself. He reads the Portuguese letters over and over. He asks Hermes to find hidden meanings. He asks Master Yalom to think like a Jewish scholar. He asks the Moor about military options. He asks Doriana about Roman history examples. He prays to any god who will help him decide.

Yet Ganga Zumba, like all of us, cannot escape who he is. And who he is now is an old, weary, and tired man. All his life he has lived in war. All his life he has known not a single day of peace. Not a single day without worrying about a Portuguese attack, not a single night without a prayer to spare his people.

And weariness and an aged body are poor counsel. The only counsel they whisper is "surrender."

Mornings of meetings, afternoons of debate, and nights of prayers succeed each other. At the end Ganga Zumba asks to speak to Doriana, the Moor, and Zumbi. They go full of hope that their pleas for no compromise are finally heard. The four of them are alone in the royal chamber now. Ganga Zumba starts.

"It is time I go in person to Recife to negotiate a treaty. I know what they want. I need to make sure we get what we want."

"Remember you represent all the people in Palmares," Doriana says.

"Moor, how are our military capabilities?" Ganga Zumba says.

"We can defend our lands from most attacks. With each graduating class, I have better officers. Princes Andala and Zumbi are ready to lead. We know the terrain. We are building weapons."

"Zumbi, are you ready to take the reins may something happen to me?"

"I am, Sire."

"I am relieved to hear that. I need a strong group behind in case there is an ambush in Recife. I want Doriana to take up as regent and Zumbi as king, if I do not return. Andala and Ganga Zona are coming with me; they know the Portuguese already."

"But, Sir, the king of Portugal is not coming to Recife."

"That is correct, I may use that as an advantage. They will be negotiating with a king. I will be negotiating with a governor who needs to offer his own king evidence of his own success. He is accountable to his king; I am to myself."

Doriana looks at Zumbi and they both look at the Moor. Ganga Zumba amends:

"And I am accountable to my family." He looks at Zumbi. "And to our people."

"Who else are you taking with you to negotiate?"

"Ganga Zona and Andala, as I said, who were there before and know their group, and I will bring Master Yalom as well."

Zumbi wants to speak but the words remain in his mouth.

***

The Portuguese governor Aires de Souza e Castro awaits the African delegation, pacing back and forth. To this last moment his advisors cannot agree on the wisdom of his huge political gamble to negotiate with escaped slaves. Their advances, conquests, and victories are his best argument. The fear in the population of an invasion of fanatic Black men, armed with machetes and swords, is spread in each tavern as a bloody nightmare.

Souza e Castro has decided to receive the delegation and does not know what to expect. Nobody knows what to expect. This has never happened before: European powers in the American colonies receiving an African delegation, one whose kingdom is also in the Americas.

The African delegation comes through Recife's streets in the morning, having spent the night in the forest surrounding Recife. King Ganga Zumba, his brother, and his son come on horseback. The king wears his Tupi royal cloak, woven by the native women using blue, red, and green macaw feathers. On his head he carries a bantu royal crown. Around his neck he wears a collar made of shark teeth, an old gift from the Goytacazes ambassadors.

It is hard to imagine the Portuguese king in such a parade, yet Ganga Zumba is a king much closer to the ground. His advisors are all Black men except for Zenaida, a Black woman, and Master Yalom, a Sephardic Jewish scholar. The group comes surrounded by the king's lictors bearing fasces and swords, they too adorned with tropical feathers, their Black skin shining in the tropical heat. It is a full display of power and dignity. If not forgotten by history, this king would count as the first truly Brazilian national leader.

The Portuguese governor waits with his cabinet, all white Portuguese men, their clothes of white and maroon linen, their feet in tall leather boots, their heads with large hats bearing long feathers, the only hint of color in their appearance. They are informed of the African delegation arrival and come to the door of the governor's mansion. Across from the mansion lies the city square.

Despite the slave owners' best efforts to hide the African delegation from the enslaved, several observe their peers in awe, and this march will feed legends and rumors for centuries to come.

Stopping in front of the governor's mansion Ganga Zumba speaks first, his voice resounding through the open square.

"We come in peace, Governor Aires de Souza e Castro!" He speaks in fluent Portuguese with a hint of Bantu accent.

The governor is startled that this man knows his name. His mind scrambles to respond.

"We receive you in peace!" he answers without conviction. The Portuguese authorities look at each other.

Ganga Zumba smiles, a broad smile that seems to illuminate the whole city. The Portuguese still do not know what to do. They remain serious, searching for words and actions to match the moment.

One energic Portuguese petit officer steps up and offers to take the king's horses by holding the reins. Ganga Zumba dismounts and so does his entourage. He is taller than most men in sight.

Governor Aires finally unfreezes and step forward, extending his right hand, which is taken by Ganga Zumba. They walk in.

"Better to take them from open view by other slaves!" whispers one Portuguese official.

They gather in the spacious conference hall, a large table its centerpiece. The governor takes a center chair and Ganga

Zumba the one across from him, with Ganga Zona and Andala sitting by each of the king's sides.

"We are here to discuss ways to contain the aggressions our troops inflict on each other," the governor begins.

"Your troops are the ones attacking our villages and communities."

"Your boys attacked Garanhuns."

"When we attacked Garanhuns, we sent your people back here alive and well and we freed the enslaved. When you attack us, you take my people prisoners in shackles. These are not equivalent."

The governor does not let up.

"You took our property. We take our pieces back."

"People are not property. These are not pieces. They are our people."

"They were sold to us in Africa. We bought them, from people just like you. They are our property. That is why we call them pieces, valuable pieces, like pieces of gold or silver." A sly smile opens on the governor's face.

Ganga Zumba stands up. The meeting appears to be over before it officially begins. The governor, wide-eyed and serious now, says, "How do you want to make any progress?"

"We need to start with some common understanding," replies Ganga Zumba, still standing.

"And what do you propose as common understanding between us?"

"We are here to discuss ways for both our peoples to live in peace in this same land."

"I can give you some land and some people, but I cannot give you all land and all people."

"What do you mean by that?"

"We can agree on territory for Africans that were born in Palmares to rule and remain free."

The fallout of that proposal does not escape Ganga Zumba. "How about those in Palmares who escaped from your chains?"

"Those shall be returned to their rightful owners."

Much like the letters proposing terms and conditions, this sentence will haunt Ganga Zumba for the coming days and nights and until his last moment of life. He looks at Ganga Zona and Andala and sees that they too are digesting the offer's meaning. It is not lost on them that each one of them was born in Palmares.

***

A few days and a Catholic mass later they reach an agreement. The two copies of the treaty signed by Ganga Zumba are marked with the royal seal of the Kingdom of Portugal, one going to Lisbon the other carried to Palmares.

The royal entourage enters the village without fanfare. The silence between them is revealing, yet no one receiving them knows the details. Only they know. And they avoid everybody's eyes, let alone questions. In front of the royal compound before dismounting, Ganga Zumba proclaims, "I have brought us peace! Peace for our time!"

The community erupts in joyful celebration. Zumbi waits for his uncle at the palace door. He smiles like everyone else, yet his eyes look at something else. He watches Doriana and Master Yalom, who fail to join in the celebrations. His smile fades into a frown. Ganga Zumba walks toward him and receives the royal truncheon from the prince. Along with all of the entourage they walk inside, heading toward the council's hall.

Silence follows them inside and anticipation grows. Ganga Zumba takes his place at the center and is given his copy of the agreement. Zumbi keeps observing Doriana and Master Yalom.

"The Portuguese agreed to respect our boundaries! These mountains in the middle will be our home forever."

This governing council has all main advisors, representatives from each of the five citadels plus those in the central government at Macaco. They know concessions on one part begets concessions on the other.

"What did we give them in return?" asks the representative from Amaro.

"We respect their property," Ganga Zumba says without conviction.

"Which property?" engages the elder.

"All property."

The incredulous elder challenges the king. "They call enslaved persons 'property.' Actually, they call them 'pieces.' Are we respecting that too?"

"Yes."

With that single yes, the room stops. Nobody speaks for a long time. Doriana and Master Yalom oscillate between looking at floor, at Zumbi, and at Ganga Zumba. The Moor, with his military training to follow orders is quiet, his single eye staring into the distance. The elder eventually continues his questioning, breaking the silence.

"What other concessions are in this treaty?"

"We must relocate Palmares."

"What?" snaps Zumbi.

"We will live in the valley of Cucaú under Portuguese protection."

Doriana intervenes. "This is like the Romans telling the port city of Carthage to relocate away from the seashore into the barren desert. Even the Carthaginians, facing utter destruction, resisted that humiliating condition."

"Yes, and thus they were utterly destroyed," answers Ganga Zumba.

"Leaving an example of honor in the face of brutal, powerful, enemies," counters Zumbi.

"This is not a treaty, this is a trap" agrees the Moor, for the first time disagreeing with the king's decision.

"We are all tired of war, and killing, and fear. It is time to concentrate on our families, our crops, and building our cities. I cannot wage war any longer. I have lost too many men. Good men. I have lost so many soldiers. I am tired of going up against an enemy that never seems to run out of ammunition while we spend time counting pellets. It is time to try another venue. It is time to engage and find a way to live side by side."

Ganga Zumba's words resound in the large hall. A few elders walk out, their heads down, among them Master Yalom. The smaller group—Zumbi, the Moor, Doriana, Ganga Zona, and Andala—remain in the room, silent. Zumbi speaks first.

"You have sold honor for peace and you will end up with neither."

Ganga Zumba avoids Zumbi's eyes for the first time in his life.

"All they sought was time to prepare. Prepare to kill us all," Zumbi concludes.

"This treaty will guarantee our land and our peace. The Portuguese will give us documents of ownership to these lands," Andala says.

"These documents are written on the same paper and with the same feather that writes ownership of our people. I hold both claims to be illegitimate," Zumbi replies.

"You hold? You hold? Who are you? Who are you to hold claims as illegitimate?" Andala says.

"I am a prince, like you. Like you, I have responsibilities to protect our people. All of them, not just a select few."

"Silence! Andala is my successor and Zumbi, you must obey," says Ganga Zumba.

"Is this what this is about? Are you shoring up your succession? If we fall to the Portuguese there will be nothing to rule over, nobody to follow your tired orders."

Kings are unused to challenge; it is their nature after a lifetime of hearing only yes. Ganga Zumba is no exception. He musters the remaining authority left in him and tries to sound commanding.

"You must respect me and follow my lead. A decision has been made."

For long minutes Zumbi takes slow, deep breaths while his mind explodes with thoughts and emotions.

"Respect is granted and can be withdrawn," he says. "Respect is earned by words and actions and as such can be lost by words and actions."

He storms out of the room and the palace, where a crowd has gathered in the plaza. The terms of the agreement are now flying like tropical birds across the forest, to every household, to all the villages. The people are quickly dividing, like the two sides of a coconut struck by a sharp sword. They fall off to each side and the sweet water inside spills out forever.

Those born in Palmares are divided. Many have parents who escaped slavery and could be facing a return to their brutal masters; they are fierce against any compromise. There is a small group, born in Palmares, whose parents were also born in Palmares; they fall into the Ganga Zumba group. This small group is the elite of the quilombo and many hold positions of power, so their voice is loud. The group of those who have fled Portuguese chains is in open revolt. They seek a leader and back Zumbi. Among them is a special group whose alliance to Zumbi is close to devotion: the families who were liberated in the attack on Garanhuns. They come to the center and form a bodyguard protecting him.

When Zumbi steps outside he is greeted by those who escaped enslavement with a new chant.

"King Zumbi! King Zumbi!"

The Moor and Doriana follow Zumbi out of the palace. Seeing them, Zumbi asks for Master Yalom.

"I have seen him leaving with the other elders," says Doriana.

"Find him and bring him here," Zumbi asks the Moor, who takes it as an order.

In a few moments the Moor returns with Master Yalom.

"Where have you been?" Zumbi says.

"I have been talking to the elders and leaders from the other villages and tribes. They agree this treaty is foolish and think Ganga Zumba is too old and tired to lead Palmares. The problem is each one of them is now seeing himself as that leader. We are running the risk of civil war."

"That is exactly what the Portuguese want: to spare them the trouble of killing us, we will do it for them," Zumbi says.

"There is only one person who can unite us all: you," Doriana says.

"I agree," says the Moor.

"I will go speak with them," Zumbi says.

"Be careful, my Lord," Doriana says.

"I can go with you," the Moor says.

"Thank you, my teacher. I must go alone. At the end of this conversation I will be either dead or king. While I am there, I need you to organize two operations. First, make sure the guards here in Macaco are loyal to you, to us. Second, send a dispatch of trusted men to secure Osenga. Andala is very influential there and his wife will for certain resist. If needed, arrest them."

The orders are clear and the Moor is a disciplined military leader.

Doriana has trembling hands waving goodbye, and before Zumbi goes, she embraces him tightly and whispers in his ear, "Remember the Roman, Lucan: make us enemies of every people on earth, but save us from civil war."

Zumbi and Pintada walk alone to the hut where the elders are gathered and where several guards from different villages are posted. They get out of his away and when he gets in the conversation stop, the elders waiting in silence for Zumbi's words. Zumbi looks at Chiamaka knowing his father-in-law will be his natural ally.

"This treaty is a mistake. My uncle, who led us through twenty-five years of progress, is now too weary to fight a war. I have no doubt the Portuguese intended exactly this response: our division. I have no doubt they do not intent to respect any agreed-upon borders and as soon as they are ready, they will take us all back into slavery. We must deny them their most devastating weapon: our disunion. We must continue to fight them with our most powerful tool: our union. The union of Palmares, from Macaco to Amaro, from Zambi to Tapera, from Osenga to Macaco, must continue." As he speaks, he looks the leader of each village in the eye.

"The world is not a province of white people. We hear accounts of brown people living in the far corners, we hear accounts of the Tupi, we hear account of Africans. There are still many corners of the world to be connected to the human village. We must be one race. We must join, not divide. And we must start here.

"The pale hands have found strength in their technology of hate. We must build on our community of love for one another. If we succeed here, we maintain the fire of hope in the hearts of Africans and Tupi on all this continent. We must succeed. If we fail here, the dream of free African hands on the American continent will continue to be postponed until one day it will be a dream for other people with different tongues. I know the dream will never die, but if we stay alive this dream will remain a reality. We have built something the Portuguese fear: a community of strong and free Africans on the American continent. Our dream is their nightmare. Let us stay together.

"I want to show you something."

Zumbi goes out and asks for ten arrows from the guards. Reluctantly, they obey. With the ten arrows he returns to the hut, carrying five arrows in each hand. He deposits five on a table and raises the others in his right hand.

"These are our five villages," he says. He gives each chief an arrow that they take uneasily. "Now you will break these arrows, one at a time, Chiamaka from Zambi, Jaha from Amaro, Haben from Tapera, and Ashon from Osenga."

"Amaro," Zumbi says, and Chief Jaha easily breaks the single arrow with his bare hands.

"Zambi." Chiamaka leaves another broken arrow.

"Tapeca." Lord Haben sends his arrow in two pieces to the floor.

187

"Osenga." Chief Ashon looks at Andala, who is quietly watching from the side, but he cannot resist Zumbi's clear and commanding voice and easily splits his arrow in two.

"Macaco." Now Zumbi looks at Andala but breaks the single arrow himself.

Then he bundles the remaining five arrows together with the string of a bow and gives them to Ashon.

"Break it."

Chief Ashon once again looks at Andala, then tries hard to break the bundle of five arrows. He cannot do it. The bundle is passed from chief to chief, and none can break the five arrows tightly bound together. Finally, they return the bundle to Zumbi.

"Together we are strong. One at a time we will be easily broken."

"Give it to me," says Andala.

He tries with no better success than any other leader to break the bundle. Finally, he throws it to the ground in frustration.

"This is silly and proves nothing," he says and storms out the room.

Zumbi picks up the bundle from the floor and holds it high with his right hand.

"This is Palmares."

Four chiefs kneel down and clap their hands while Ashon, like Andala, leaves the room. Pintada roars. Even the crowd outside is now quiet, waiting for the outcome of negotiations.

Zumbi comes out, the five-arrow bundle in his right hand. He raises it. Someone hands him green and yellow colors to paint his face. When someone asks him what the colors represent, Zumbi does not hesitate.

"The green is for our forests, and the yellow for our gold."

"Gold? We do not have any gold."

"Our gold is the African people."

From that moment on, the symbol of Zumbi's right hand holding five arrows becomes the symbol of free Palmares, to be used on shields and in places of gathering. The colors green and yellow become the colors of Palmares. With his hand raised holding those very arrows, and his face painted with green and yellow, he speaks to the people crowded in the central plaza.

"Peace was never an option. For those who only see us as slaves, peace is never an option. Appeasement with those who hate us can only result in our death and destruction. We will resist. As long as there is air to breathe in my body there will be no agreement short of emancipation of all Black people. Whenever there is one of us in chains, our people is in chains. When we accept those compromises, we accept defeat and humiliation. And when I look at you, I do not see a defeated people. I see a strong, smart, hardworking, and determined people—a people determined to make this land, where many of us were born, our home.

"We are now Americans. This is our home and nobody will take us back to chains. You have heard me say no to those who want to keep you down. Now I want to say yes to standing up, yes to sharing these lands with the Tupi, and, if the Portuguese agree to treat us as equals, with them as well. I say yes, to justice and equality of all under the law. I say yes, to recognizing the talent and hard work of all. I say yes, to a level playfield where we can all compete on equal footing.

"Most importantly, I say yes to you. Whoever you are, if you come in peace and acceptance of all, you are my brother, and you are my sister. Anyone, no matter what creed or color, can have a home in Palmares. If you are willing to make yourself useful to your neighbor you have a place here. I say yes to you."

"Yes! Yes to Palmares! Always!" replies the crowd. "Zumbi, king of Palmares. Zumbi, king of America," they chant.

Somewhere in the crowd one voice speaks to a neighbor. "To love a king is not bad, but to have a king who loves you is better."

***

Moving to Cucaú

Still, some people want to follow Ganga Zumba; still, some people want to abide by an agreement that promises chains to so many. And still, Ganga Zumba is Zumbi's uncle, the one who took him in his arms as a baby and who raised him. Zumbi orders no harm be done to any of them. They are to be given the right to settle somewhere else, even if it is in a valley surrounded by Portuguese farmers and troops.

About a thousand families, most from Osenga, elect to follow Ganga Zumba and his group. This is a small minority of Palmares' families, but it bleeds Zumbi's heart to see them go. The group departs in a somber mood without celebration. The children express their emotions to see their friends leaving while the adults pretend they are still one nation.

Zumbi moves into the royal compound at the center of Macaco. The Republic of Palmares has a new leader and does not recognize treaties signed with the Portuguese unless slavery is abolished and all Africans emancipated.

"The truth is the other way around, Zumbi" says Master Yalom. "The Portuguese do not recognize the free Republic of Palmares until slavery is extended to these mountains and all Africans are in chains."

"That being the case, Master, we are at war."

The Occult History of Africa

The occult history of Africa is the occult history of all humanity. From minerals in its soil, life grew into plants; from that green grass and those giant trees sprouted animals clothed in leather and movement. The oldest gods were African gods. Here they molded man and woman on the shores of Lake Tana, from which water flows to create the Nile River. Here man and woman made their first home and their first offspring. Here the first stage was set for the immortal acts of love and murder that shaped human civilization.

From Africa, men and women spread around the terrestrial sphere in search of peace but carrying with them the seeds of war. From the savannah we moved to the desert, from the desert to the mountains, from the mountains to the steppes, where we crossed a bridge made of ice to find America. From America men and women jumped to the moon.

Always searching for that promised peace and love, only finding war and hate.

And so, all human history is African history.

All living humans trace their ancestry back to the Black continent. Our collective longing is for something we one day had at our cradle: that love and peace we crave.

And one day when we finally find the way back home, we will be walking, for the last time, under an African sun.

And seeing Africa for the first time.

In Lieu of an Explanation

Fiction is history that might have happened. History is fiction that did happen.
—André Gide in *The Counterfeiters*

This is a work of fiction composed with a lot of imagination and based on true, magnificent historic events: the story of Palmares and of Zumbi, a story that has fascinated generations of Brazilians. This story certainly fascinated me, and as a Brazilian living in the United States I have always wanted to share it with Americans in general and African Americans in particular. The challenge is that we do not have reliable information about what life was like in this, the greatest quilombo in the history of Brazil and likely in the Americas.

Zumbi, the African King of Brazil is thus a work of historical fiction as much as a labor of love. Apart from the known actual people, events, and locales, all names, characters, places, and incidents, are the product of the author's imagination or used fictitiously. Any resemblance to current events of actual locales or to living persons is entirely coincidental. Or, one could say, the product of the reader's imagination …

I am not a historian but a psychiatrist by training, and it's clear to me this book is made up of my own obsessions, including: Brazil, the majestic green continent, the fight against prejudice and discrimination, Ancient Rome, and the history of science.

We have precious few historical facts about Palmares. These are my anchors. What happened in between these facts is what I have tried to fill with imagination. It is fact that there was a huge community of free Africans living in the Northeast of Brazil between the early 1600s and 1695, basically for a century. The visit described in Chapter 12 where Ganga Zumba visits Recife as a king is also in the historical record, though I imagined the details and dialogue. Most importantly, there was a prince of Palmares named Zumbi who took power after Ganga Zumba, and he did lead a fierce resistance against the Portuguese forces.

The major challenge is that all we know about Zumbi and Palmares comes from Portuguese or European sources (there are some letters from Dutch explorers). These sources are obviously biased and prejudiced against the African presence. There was explicit need to demoralize and dehumanize Africans, for they were there to be exploited as enslaved persons. I don't think we can accept the observations of the Portuguese as valid and we don't have any records written by the Africans. That's where imagination is necessary. I humbly offer mine, and I hope I can bring others along to imagine an alternative narrative. It's possible, and I hope this book will be proof of that.

The names of Zumbi's children, like so many facts surrounding him, are unknown or the product of speculation. As such, I agonized for days about which tradition to follow or which names to use. Since I had thought about two fictional children and the real Zumbi supposedly had three children with his African wife, I needed five names. As I was holding this internal debate, I read a column by the Brazilian journalist Thiago Amparo, "Utopia for Black Children," about children killed by police violence in Rio de Janeiro (published in Folha de Sao Paulo May 25, 2020). In it, he writes about six children who died in 2019 after being caught in the crossfire in Rio de Janeiro. They were: *Joao Pedro* Matos Pinto (14), Jennifer *Cilene* Gomez (11), *Kauan* Peixoto (12), Agatha *Felix* (8), *Kauá* Rosario (11), Kethellen *Umbelino* Oliveira Gomes (5). I immediately saw in them Zumbi's children, and that's how Joao Pedro, Cilene, Kauan, Felix, and Umbelino sprouted in my imagination.

This work of historical fiction is inspired by many other authors including Marguerite Yourcenar, Robert Harris, Robert Graves, Irvin Yalom (the inspiration for Master Yalom), and of course, Dame Hilary Mantel. They've all made me a happy reader. If I can give the reader a fraction of the pleasure I've had reading them, I am a happy author.

Languages Used

English is my second language and I am not sure Portuguese is still my first. This book was written as a daily effort in English and Portuguese, for my goal has been to release this novel in both languages simultaneously.

Zumbi: Left and Right

It's inevitable that historical figures fall prey to interpretation using the political dichotomy of left and right with which we live in the highly charged early twenty-first century. Zumbi is no exception.

When I was growing up, in the seventies in Brazil, Zumbi was appropriated by the "left wing" as a symbol of rebellion "against the oppressor" in colonial times—as if Zumbi had been a proto-Marxist Latin-American guerilla fighter a la Castro. This myth was constructed in part by a narrative that Zumbi was raised by a Portuguese friar who would have instilled in him the liberal values of Western civilization. The more I read about this narrative, the more it sounded to me as a colonial reading of a mythological figure for whom we have precious few historical data. As always, we fill the blanks of the historical record with our own prejudices. The story of Zumbi as raised by Catholic friars sounded to me akin to that type of colonial mindset, as if Africans would be unable to create their own civilization or organize their own society. I reject this perspective.

More recently in Brazil, Zumbi has also been re-interpreted by the "right wing" as an expression of the times, in part by accusing him of having slaves of his own. It is important to note that all documentation we have available about Palmares comes from Portuguese sources who obviously would be interested in spreading the news to existing slaves that Palmares offered them no hope but continued enslavement. You may call this an example of seventeenth century "fake news." I reject this perspective as well.

The main problem I have with either interpretation is that both "wings" offer their version as the historical truth. Here again we divert. My Zumbi is an imagined character based on the few historical events we have beyond dispute. There was a large quilombo in Alagoas/Pernambuco between approximately 1605 and November of 1695; there were multiple failed expeditions to destroy it; there was a military leader known as Zumbi who was thought of as having magical powers; there was a peace proposal that lead to Ganga Zumba's death followed by Zumbi's ascension. These are facts reported in letters to the king of Portugal preserved by the Overseas Archives in Portugal. These letters also attest to the concern Palmares represented to the court in Lisbon. These are historical facts. What we imagine happened between those lines is what this book is about.

I choose to believe this nation of African men and women were able to create an alternative society in the tropics. I choose to believe this story deserves to be known as well as the Spartacus revolt in Rome, which lasted for a couple of years several decades before Jesus walked the earth and has received so much more attention, and as well as Wallace's revolt in Scotland, which was shorter in duration and longer in imagery. These revolts are expressions of the power of people to resist oppression. What did Spartacus's revolt and Wallace's movement have in common that Palmares did not have? They were led by White men.

If the world needs a classical hero who is a Black man, it needs to get acquainted with Zumbi of Palmares.

NOTES ON
SELECTED CHAPTERS

Chapter 1: A New Hope

The benediction for Zumbi's birth was constructed as the opposite of the curse placed on Bento Spinoza by the Jewish leadership in Amsterdam that same year. This episode is reported in the Dutch interlude at the end of the chapter using the version I found in Will Durant's *Story of Philosophy*. The song cited is "You are the Sunshine of my Life" by Stevie Wonder. The character Djavan Wonder is a double homage to the African American musical genius of Stevie Wonder and the African Brazilian musical genius of Djavan.

Chapter 3: The Education of a Prince

I've always found fascinating how the Middle Ages grouped subjects in the trivium and quadrivium. The final quip on Aristotle is a modification of the answer given to an African American student and described in *Between the World and Me* by Ta-Nehisi Coates; in his telling the question is about Tolstoy.

Chapter 5: First Love for a Prince

In this chapter I've used a classical poem from Brazilian literature, "I-Juca-Pirama" by Goncalves Ledo. This is a poem that school-aged children in Brazil, myself included, had to memorize. In this chapter I also reference the novel *Iracema* based on the character of the same name by Jose de Alencar, another great Brazilian author from the 1800s, though I changed the name to read *America* backwards. In the process of researching this novel I've encountered a translation of *Iracema* by Isabel Burton, freely available online now.

Chapter 7: The Attack of 1667

Those who follow Roman history will easily recognize Cesar's strategy in Alesia. The use of slings is also historical to ancient Rome, including the whistling sling bullets.

Chapter 8: Initiation

Those interested in hermetic traditions will recognize here the seven principles described in the 1908 book *The Kybalion*, published anonymously. I've also added a little hermetic spin to Plato's allegory of the cave.

Chapter 9: The Battle of Garanhuns

The blessing given by the priest is the *Prayer to Saint George for Strong Protection Against Enemies* as found on the site catholictruth.net, a prayer that also can be heard in popular songs in Brazil. St. George is known in English-speaking countries as the patron saint of England and he is also so claimed by Ethiopia, Georgia, Greece, Lithuania, Palestine, Portugal, and Russia.

Chapter 10: Nights at the Circus

This is a special chapter to me due to its being a complete fruit of imagination. I just could not get out of my head this encounter. It's important to know that I have taken a few licenses with history in this chapter, namely that the circus as we know it was invented a few centuries later, in the 1700s and 1800s, and while the Portuguese would indeed bring the ukulele to Hawaii they would do so in the 1800s as well. The Portuguese music style *fado* was also created much later.

What I wanted to create in this chapter was a completely magical narrative.

Chapters 12 Royal Weddings

The poem cited is from a Robert Browning poem from the 1800s. Poetic license is invoked, justified by its beauty.

Domingos Jorge Velho was known for brutality and violence even in an age where brutality and violence were commonplace. The episode used to illustrate his brutality was taken from descriptions of the massacre at Béziers, France, on July 22, 1209, the first major military action of the Albigensian Crusade which aimed at eradicating a group known as Cathars.

The line about removing wings from flies came to memory from descriptions of Roman Emperor Domitian.

***

If you want to know the real history, there are several books on Palmares in general and Zumbi in particular, though most are available in Portuguese only. One great introduction to the history in English is *Quilombo dos Palmares, Brazil's Lost Nation of Fugitive Slaves* by Glenn Alan Cheney.

In Portuguese you may read *Zumbi, O Ultimo Heroi dos Palmares* by Carla Caruso (available in e-book); *O Quilombo dos Palmares* by Edison Carneiro; *Palmares: A Guerra dos Escravos* by Decio Freitas; *Zumbi dos Palmares: Historias, Simbolos, e Memoria* by Flavio Gomes; and *Palmares: Mito e Romance da Utopia Brasileira* by Carlos Diegues and Everardo Rocha.

A great YouTube channel where you can check out stories from Brazilian history is "Buenas Ideias" by Eduardo Bueno.

ACKNOWLEDGMENTS

Everything I do I owe to the patience, kindness, and love from my wife and children who put up with my writing and even read my early drafts.

My parents caused me to read from an early age and to plan a simultaneous edition in Portuguese.

This book, that is a long-standing dream, came to be with the support of many friends and colleagues who read and commented on its early drafts, first among them Paulette Mehta.

My gratitude goes to my wonderful beta-readers: Sharanda Williams, Sheridan Richards, and Cheryl Batts.

Professional copyediting from Julie Miller – The Editorial Department – cleared the text from my English as a second language missteps.

The Spanish artist Andres Aguirre created the map and the family tree illustrations.

To the many wonderful history and literature teachers of the world I leave my sincere recognition. This book owns its existence to your work.

ABOUT THE AUTHOR

Erick Maia was born in Brazil and lives in the United States. He is the recipient of the 2020 Dr. Edith Irby Jones Excellence in Diversity and Inclusion – Middle/Senior Career Faculty Award. *Zumbi, The African King of Brazil* is his debut novel.

TOTAL WARFARE:
DOMINGOS JORGE VELHO

For the first years of his life he does not speak any words, and when he eventually does he speaks a mix of Portuguese, Tupi, and Spanish. For the most part he prefers silence—angry silence. From those very first years he also brings forward a deep anger at the world, at people, at their voices and their constant nagging. From those very early years he knows one solution to that noise and nagging: violence. He convinces himself he must kill something every day, be it a bird, a lizard, or eventually a person. When he does not kill, he maims; as a child he captures flies and removes their wings, watching with joy as the hapless creatures run around clumsily. Creatures of the air struggle on the ground; he, a creature of war, struggles in peaceful times.

There is only one profession open to such a man: hunting of native Tupi and escaped Africans. He excels at it. His skill remains one: violence.

He favors attacking villages away from Portuguese settlements. Even those barely civilized Europeans are too delicate for him. Those men and women, used to the harsh environment of caravels and Atlantic storms, are appalled by his manners. His troops fear him and know to obey him without question. Their bounty is plenty and so their questions are few anyway.

During one incursion the Tupi hide in a Jesuit church, where maybe the cross and the savior of pale hands will defend them. He decides to make this one village an example to undermine future resistance. He orders them all slaughtered. When his lieutenant suggests that they should separate and spare those who are converts to the Lord, he counters:

"Kill them all. The Lord will know his own."

He is perfect for his age and his fortune grows from his first missions of capturing Tupi men for farm work in the hinterlands to capturing whole villages for pillage. His name is now legend in the northeast region where the Tupi think he is Portuguese, the Portuguese say he is a barbarian Brazilian, and those born in Brazil say he is a demon. To amuse himself, and annoy others, when asked where he is from he answers, "from hell."

One day, when the Governor of Pernambuco decides to end Palmares once and for all, there is one name to call upon. For the fiercest of games, the roughest of predators.

His name is Domingos Jorge Velho.